Stories Written on COVID Walls

Melissa R. Mendelson

Contents

THE COVID TOUCH

Mother Nature was as screwed up as the country. Couldn't call it fake news when the snowflakes covered the lawn in May. The snow didn't help the porch either. Another board snapped apart.

The truck took forever to start, but Kirk finally peeled out of the driveway. He slammed on the brakes and backed onto his neighbor's lawn, crushing the sign that read, "Stay Inside and Save Lives." He smiled as the sign moaned and bent under his tires. He slammed on the gas, leaving tire marks in the snow.

He had a few errands to run. First stop was the gas station. He pulled behind a station wagon and saw a woman wearing a mask and gloves.

"Come on. You're just pumping gas." Kirk honked at her. She flipped him off and finished putting gas in her car. "Fucking bitch," he snarled when the station wagon finally drove off. "Wasting my damn time." He stepped out of the car and popped the covering to the gas tank open.

"Can you believe those protests yesterday?" An old man stood on the other side of the pump. He wasn't wearing gloves, but he had a mask on. "Damn stupid people if you ask me."

"Nobody asked you." Kirk leaned against his truck, waiting for the tank to fill up.

"They think the virus isn't real. On top of that, they're marching with skull masks and rifles. What kind of shit is that?" The old man lifted the nozzle and put it into his mini car. "Don't they get the situation we're in here? We're all dying."

"Not you." Kirk turned and spat on the ground near the man's feet. "My wife and friends and I were at that protest. The virus is fake."

"It's real! You're going to kill us all!"

"Pull your head out of your liberal ass." Kirk put the pump back in place and closed the gas cap. "It's people like you who will do us in." He licked his lips. "'Scuse me," he said, stepping away. He needed a cigarette, especially after talking to that moron.

"Aren't you going to move your truck up?" The man asked.

Kirk looked back and saw someone waiting. He glanced at the old man who looked like he was going to burst into tears. Kirk took another step away and then cursed under his breath. He stormed into his truck, revved the engine, nearly backed into the waiting car, and peeled into the parking spot outside the store.

"Asshole!" the old man screamed.

Kirk stormed into the gas station and nodded a curt hello to the pimple-faced twerp behind the counter. He grabbed a pack of Twizzlers and waited in line. There were two people in front of him, both with masks over their faces. He rolled his eyes and shook his head but bit his tongue.

"Nest," the twerp said with a lisp.

One idiot left, and the other checked out. Again, he rolled his eyes, tempted to push the person out of the way.

"Nest," the twerp repeated, avoiding eye contact with Kirk.

"Two packs. Marlboro. And these Twizzlers." He looked out the window to the car he almost backed into. It was still at the pump, and the driver was nowhere to be seen. "Where the hell did they go?"

"Eighteen," the twerp said, holding out his hand.

Kirk slapped a twenty-dollar bill into his hand, hard. He glanced away only for a second before turning back to see the twerp was gone. "What the hell?" He leaned over the counter, but there was no sign of him. "Where'd he go? Fine. Keep the fucking two dollars." He yelled into the empty space, grabbed his cigarettes and Twizzlers, and walked outside.

He needed to grab some meat at the supermarket before there was a shortage. His wife also demanded ice cream. Thank God she couldn't get pregnant. He didn't need to deal with any rug rats, especially with the way the country was today.

"Wear a mask," a woman shrieked at him as he walked in. "Where's the manager? He's not wearing a mask. He needs to wear a mask."

"Jesus, lady. Shut your piehole."

"You're going to kill us all." She dropped her groceries on the floor and ran.

"Crazy bitch." Kirk sifted through the groceries on the floor and picked out a few items. "But thank you for your insanity."

He was about to step away when he heard a graveling voice. "You can't be in here without a mask."

"I can't what?" He turned to see a heavyset man with a long beard. "I don't see you wearing a mask."

"I am." The man struggled to pull his mask away. He ripped a few beard hairs in the process. "Put a mask on or get out."

Kirk sighed. He placed the items he was holding on the floor. He pulled off his coat, then his black t-shirt. He wrapped the t-shirt around his face and tucked it below his eyes. Then, he put his coat back on, zippering it up close to his neck. "Better," he spat, glaring at the man and picking up his items.

The bearded man knelt and gathered the things Kirk touched but didn't take. "It's people like you that will end us."

"It's people like you th—" The man had disappeared. "What? Where did he go? He was right there."

Kirk backed away. He rubbed his chin and shook his head. He had to get the ice cream.

He grabbed a carton of vanilla fudge and hurried to the line, ignoring the stares he got. Did he make that man disappear? Nah. That was ridiculous. He just walked away. He rubbed his chin again. Yes, that man walked away.

The cashier touched the items Kirk placed on the conveyor belt, but she was wearing plastic gloves. Still, she didn't disappear. See? He didn't make that man disappear. Bagging his groceries, Kirk dropped a pack of cookies onto the floor.

"Sir, your cookies." The woman behind him bent down and picked them up. He went to take them from her, but she was gone, the cookies crashing to the floor.

"What did you do?" The cashier screamed.

"I... I didn't do nothing." He grabbed the cookies and the rest of his items. People were staring at him, their faces filled with panic. "Stop looking at me like that. I didn't do nothing," he said and hurried out of the store.

He shivered as he hurried to his truck. Fuck, he was cold, and it was May. It wasn't supposed to be cold now, but things were so fucked up. They really were, and he still had a few stops left to make. But he wanted to head home and check on his wife. They didn't have the best of times, but he still loved her.

When he pulled into the driveway, his heart dropped. The front door was wide open.

"Georgia? Georgia, where are you?" He dropped the groceries in the kitchen and checked downstairs. She wasn't there. "Georgia, damn you. Answer me right now."

"Up here," came her meek voice from the bedroom.

"Are you still in bed? It's the afternoon already."

Kirk flew up the stairs. He opened his bedroom door and found Georgia sitting on the floor, drenched in tears. In front of her were pictures of her parents. They didn't live too far from them, and Georgia had muttered something earlier about going to see them.

"Did you see your parents?" Georgia slowly nodded. "Then why in the fuck are you crying like a baby?"

"They're gone," she cried. "They're both... Gone."

"Jesus, Georgia. If you saw them, how are they both gone?" He leaned down toward her but didn't touch her.

"After I hugged my father at the door, he disappeared. I ran to my mother and grabbed hold of her. She disappeared. They're gone, Kirk. I killed my parents."

"Jesus. You sound insane."

"I touched them!"

Her words felt like ice in his throat. "Maybe you were hallucinating."

She grabbed his arm, and he stumbled back. "You're still here. Why can't I make you disappear? I rather you be gone than my parents." She flinched as Kirk raised his hand, but he didn't strike her. "We should not have gone to that protest yesterday."

"That has nothing to do with it. Go call your parents. I'm sure they're home." He turned away from her.

"I did! The phone keeps ringing. They're not answering. They're dead, Kirk. They are dead. Because of me."

"Bullshit."

The phone on the nightstand rang. Georgia screamed. Kirk raised his hand but then lowered it, muttering under his breath. The phone rang again, and with each ring Georgia grew more pale. Kirk growled and snapped the receiver from the cradle.

"If this is Georgia's parents, and you are playing some sick, fucking game, I am not playing along."

"Kirk?"

"Bobby?" Kirk asked into the receiver.

"They're gone."

"Gone? Who's gone? You sound kind of funny."

"I kissed my wife good morning today," Bobby said.

"Right."

"She disappeared, Kirk. Right in front of me."

"Not you too. What did we come in contact with at the protest yesterday?"

"I checked on the boys."

"And?"

"As soon as I touched them, they disappeared. Even the fucking cat is gone."

"Bobby, slow down. Your family is not gone." Kirk heard a harsh snap, like a hammer being cocked back. "Bobby, what are you doing?"

"We should have listened. Now, the world is going to pay for our ignorance."

"Jesus, Bobby. I have known you since high school, so please don't be this stupid. You are not this stupid." No answer. "Bobby? Bobby, answer me. Answer me."

A gunshot thundered through the phone. Georgia screamed again. Kirk dropped the receiver, and it slammed against the floor.

"Call him back," Georgia whispered. "Call him back."

Kirk stared down at the phone on the floor.

"Call him back," Georgia screamed. "Call them all back! Now!"

"Shut up!" Kirk lifted the phone and dialed Bobby's number. "Come on, Bobby. Come on." The phone was ringing, and he sighed with relief. "It's ringing," he said.

"Thank God." Georgia finally breathed, but the look on Kirk's face made her gasp. "What? What is it?"

Kirk pushed the speaker button.

"We're sorry," a voice said. "You have reached a number that has been disconnected or is no longer in service."

LITTLE BIRDS WITH BROKEN WINGS

Millie slammed her laptop closed, her head bent forward. She sobbed, then wiped her tears away. She turned her chair around and grabbed a tissue off her desk. The sound of blowing her nose echoed around her bedroom. She struggled to stop crying, but she could not stop.

Her hand shook as she grabbed her cell phone off her desk. She cursed herself for being such a baby, for letting them do what they did. How could they be so cruel in a time like this?

"Fucking kids," she texted. "Fucking bullies. Did you see what they posted about me?" She saw her message was delivered. No response. "Are you there? Hello?"

"What?" Her brother texted back. "You shouldn't give a shit about what they posted about you. Not now. Not with this."

"How do I go back to school after what they did?"

"Simple. You're not."

"You're no help," Millie texted.

"I'm in New Jersey. I'm not working. Everyone's dealing with their shit. Just deal with it."

"Fine. How's your girlfriend doing?"

"What do you care? You don't like her."

"I don't," she typed.

"How's Mom and Dad?"

"Dad's out. Mom's her usual."

"He shouldn't be outside."

"He won't listen to me."

"I have to go. I'll call later," her brother texted.

"I love you." Message delivered. No response.

Why did he have to be such a jerk? They were close once, and then he met *her*. He changed. He moved to New Jersey to live with her, and now he was stuck there. Would she ever see him again?

Millie tossed her cell phone onto the desk and looked at her laptop. Assholes. The world was in chaos, and bullies were tearing her down. They should be more concerned with themselves, with surviving this virus.

How long would her father be outside? Where had he gone? It wasn't after twelve yet. Maybe he ran to the grocery store. Still, he should not be outside. If she could drive, she would have gone and gotten what he needed. He would have stayed inside where he was safe. What if he brought the virus to their home?

Millie pulled herself away from her desk and opened her bedroom door. The house was quiet. After her brother left, the house became really quiet. Her mother either sat in front of the television set or checked out the home network shopping websites on her iPad. She had no concept of reality. She had no idea money was tight.

Millie's father no longer worked, and he had cut into his savings to ensure that they had everything they needed. What they really needed was that check from the government. If that check was really being sent out, her mother was ready to spend it.

Her mother rarely washed or dried the dishes, and they were piling up in the sink. Millie's father never did the dishes. She used to take turns with her brother. Now, it was all on her.

She went downstairs and washed the dishes, placing them gently on a dish towel nearby. Mid-wash, she looked at her neighbor's house. Sometimes, she watched a young woman wash her dishes. Sometimes, the young woman acknowledged her.

Her neighbor looked up. Half of her face was swollen, her skin purplish-blue. Her left eye was shut, and her lips chapped. Her gaze met Millie's, and she dropped a plate. Tears streamed from her right eye. She grabbed the blinds and slammed them down.

"Wait," Millie screamed. "What the hell happened?" Millie waited for the blinds to be raised, but they remained down. "Come on," she muttered as she finished washing the last dish. She dried the dishes, constantly looking out the window. "What happened to your face?"

Millie checked the garbage in the kitchen. No surprise. It was full. Tomorrow was garbage pickup. She changed the bag and took the full one outside. A lot of garbage sat in front of her neighbor's house.

Millie moved slowly to the house next door. She looked around and then over at the garbage. It looked like normal garbage, but then she saw a black cord. A handset was underneath it.

The front door opened, and a large man stepped outside. He lit a cigarette, and she caught a glimpse of his bruised knuckles. He stared Millie down. She backed away as he blew an ugly cloud of smoke into the air and stepped back into the house. He slammed the front door shut.

Millie walked into her house and found her mother in the living room, sitting on the couch with the iPad on her lap. A woman turned over a fancy pocketbook on the screen. Her mother fumbled with her wallet. Was she really going to spend their savings on that?

"Mom!" Her mother looked at Millie. "Seriously? A fucking pock-etbook?"

"They're almost sold out."

"We need the money. For food. Toilet paper, if you can find it. How much is it?"

"Oh, there's a payment plan. Eighty dollars a month."

"You can't."

"Millie, it's my money."

Millie moved closer, but she stopped after stepping on the carpeting. "It's our money, Mom. Do you know where Dad is right now?"

"Outside."

"Yeah. He's out, buying things for us."

"I don't need his permission."

"No. You need your head examined." Millie was ignored as her mother entered in her credit card information. "Something happened to our neighbor," Millie said.

"Mind your business. It has nothing to do with us."

"You didn't see her face. I did. It's bad."

"Millie, I need to finish ordering this pocketbook before your father gets home."

"I don't know why I even bother."

Millie walked into the kitchen. She looked out the window at her neighbor's house. The blinds were back up, but there was no sign of the young woman.

"She can't call for help," she said to herself. "Damn it, Dad. Where the hell are you?" She looked at the phone on the kitchen wall. "What if he is hitting her again? What if he kills her?"

"9–1–1. What's your emergency?"

"I think something happened to my neighbor."

"Can you be more specific?"

"I don't know. Her face is badly bruised. One eye is shut."

"Was she attacked?"

"I don't know. I think maybe her husband did it. I saw bruises on his knuckles."

"When did you see bruises on his knuckles?"

Millie rubbed the back of her head. "A few minutes ago. Outside."

"Okay. I am dispatching a squad car. Can you confirm your address?"

"Their address. It's 214 Ranch Street."

"Okay. Squad car is on route. Can I have your name, please?"

Millie hung up the phone. She stared at it for a moment and then hurried upstairs to her bedroom. Her mother was still in the living room on her iPad. She looked out her window. Her father's car pulled into the driveway. A moment later, a squad car parked in front of her neighbor's house. Two police officers stepped outside and knocked on their door.

"Millie, want to help unload these groceries?" Her father asked from downstairs.

"Okay." Millie looked out the window again. She did the right thing. She knew she did the right thing.

"Did your mother buy something?" Her father asked as he finished bringing in the bags.

"A pocketbook. Wash your hands," Millie said.

"After we put the groceries away." She heard the anger in his voice. "Until we get those government checks, we're really tight on money. Do I want to ask how much it was?"

"Eighty dollars, I think. A month." She watched her father shake his head, avoiding eye contact with her. If she had the money, she would give it to him, but she was only fifteen. She didn't work. "I'm sorry, Dad."

"It's not your fault." He looked at her. His eyes were a mix of sadness and anger. "She just doesn't get it. She doesn't realize how bad it is out there, and it's going to get worse."

A loud knock fell on the front door. More knocks followed.

"Now what?" Her father opened the front door and came face-to-face with the police officers. He stepped outside, closing the door behind him, but left it open enough for Millie to hear what they were saying.

"We don't appreciate prank calls right now," one officer said.

"We're in the middle of a crisis. Doesn't your kid realize that?" The other officer asked.

"I'm really sorry, officers. I just got home, so I wasn't aware of any of this."

"Dad!" Millie threw open the front door. "It wasn't a prank call. He hit her. I saw her face."

"She's not home."

"That's bullshit. I was doing the dishes, and so was she. We looked at each other, and I saw her face."

"Millie," her father said. "Enough."

"No. He hit her, Dad. He really hit her."

"She's at her sister's," the second officer said.

"Did you even go in the house?"

The first officer stared at her. "We did. We looked around, but he was the only one there."

"Probably because he has her in the basement."

"Millie, go in the house." Her father gave her a stern look, and she stormed back inside. "I'm sorry, officers. It won't happen again."

"She's lucky he's not pressing charges."

Millie laughed.

"Let's go," the first officer said as he moved away from the door.

"Damn it, Millie. What were you thinking?" Her father slammed the front door shut. "Calling the cops? Now? In a time like this? It's bad enough that I have to deal with your mother, but now I have to deal with you?"

"I'm sorry. But I saw her. I saw what he did to her."

"It's not our problem." He watched a tear run down Millie's face. "Look, I know that's harsh, but right now, we have to focus on us. We have to survive. Okay?"

"What if he kills her? What if he killed her?"

"Let's hope he doesn't, but no matter what, do not call the police again. Do you understand me?"

"Yes, Dad. I understand." Millie wiped the tear away. "You need to wash your hands."

"Yes, I do, and so do you."

"I'll wash my hands upstairs. Do you want lunch?"

"In an hour. Go wash your hands."

Millie went into the upstairs bathroom and washed her hands with warm water and soap. She looked at herself in the mirror. Her brown hair was a mess. Her eyes were red from crying earlier and just now. Her skin was dry, and zit stricken. The kids at school called her ugly. They called her Silly Millie. One boy even called her Pissy. Those kids were so cruel, and even at home, those kids got to her through social media. She looked in the mirror again, but she didn't see herself. She saw her neighbor.

Millie entered her bedroom and looked at her closed laptop. She grabbed the sketchpad off her dresser and sketched her neighbor's face. She covered every detail. The bruised skin. The shut left eye. Her broken lips. Her pain and misery shining in the right eye with tears on her cheek. Was she still alive?

Millie listened to her parents arguing downstairs. Her father was trying to make her mother cancel her purchase. Her mother refused. He caved in on one condition. She had to give him her credit card. Their argument escalated, and Millie flinched when her mother screamed.

"Don't cut my credit card up," she shrieked.

"That was your last purchase. You're lucky we'll barely get by on what you left us."

"I'll use your card."

"No. You won't. I'll hide them. Now, do you want lunch?"

"I'm not hungry." Her mother stormed up the stairs. She looked in Millie's bedroom and glared at Millie. "Rat," she said and walked into her bedroom, slamming the door shut.

"Millie. Lunch," her father called from downstairs.

"Coming!" She looked at her drawing and closed the sketchpad. She slid it under the bed. Just to keep it safe.

Millie's father warmed up two English muffins, one for him and one for Millie. Millie boiled hot water for their tea. Neither one said anything. Her father took out a newspaper and read it at the kitchen table.

"It's getting worse," her father said.

"Don't go back out. It's not safe."

"I'm the only one that can. Your brother's not here."

"No. He's with her." She finished drinking her tea.

"Your mother doesn't get it." Her father drank his tea.

"She doesn't want to get it," Millie muttered. "I don't understand her."

A loud knock came from the front door. Her father looked at her. She was going to say she didn't call the police again but said nothing. She watched her father open the front door.

Their neighbor with the bruised knuckles stood outside. "We're out of toilet paper," he said.

"Excuse me?"

"I'm out of toilet paper. Seeing how your kid called the cops on me for no reason, I would say you owe me."

"Where's your wife?" Millie now stood next to her father.

"At her sister's." He snarled at Millie. "You never saw her today."

"I did see her. She dropped a plate."

"I dropped a plate. Now, how about ten rolls of toilet paper?"

"I'll give you two. If it's just you, then that should be enough." Millie's father stepped in front of her. "Two rolls."

"Go get them."

"Millie, get this man two rolls."

"Dad!"

"Now, Millie."

She stormed to the garage and opened a pack of toilet paper. She took out two rolls. Millie was about to hand them to her neighbor, but she pulled them back. "Where's your wife?" She asked.

"Here." Millie's father grabbed the toilet paper from her and shoved it into the neighbor's hands. "Don't come back."

"Keep your kid away from me." Their neighbor walked away.

"Dad, what were you thinking? We need that."

"He's still our neighbor, and you called the cops on him."

"You don't believe me. Do you?" She hurried up the stairs.

"What are you doing?"

She ran back down with the sketchbook. "Look," she said, flipping to the page with her neighbor's face. "This is what I saw today."

"Jesus," her father muttered. "But he said she's not there."

"He's lying. He did something to her."

"It doesn't matter." He handed the sketchpad to her. "There's a crisis going on, and we have to focus on that."

"What about her?" Millie asked, holding her drawing up.

"We can't save her. I'm sorry." Her father touched her on the shoulder and then moved away.

"That's it?" She asked, but her father didn't answer her.

Millie spent the afternoon in her room. She sketched her neighbor's bruised knuckles. She sketched the police officers at her front door. The toilet paper clutched in ugly, misshaped hands.

She looked out the window and saw her neighbor exit his house. He pulled his car out of the driveway and took off down the road. Where was he going?

She threw her sneakers on and headed downstairs. Her father was sitting in the family room, watching the news. She couldn't bring herself to watch the news. It was terrible. Her mother was still in her bedroom with the door closed. Millie opened the front door and stepped outside.

"Dad, I'll be right back." She left before her father could answer her.

The front door to their neighbor's house was locked, and she looked back to see if her father was watching her. She waited a moment but didn't see him. He was still probably busy watching the news. She moved around to the back of the house. She opened the gate and tried the side door, but it was also locked.

The young woman appeared and opened the door. She glanced around and looked at Millie. Her face was badly bruised, and her nose was bleeding.

"You shouldn't be here," she said.

"Are you okay? I can call the police again."

"No! Don't. I'm okay."

"You don't look okay. I know he did this to you. I saw his knuckles."

"I have nowhere to go." She stepped outside, moved back in, but then inched outside again. "I have to stay here."

"What about your sister?"

"My sister lives in Florida. How am I going to get there?"

"Then come to my house. You can stay with me." Millie surprised her by touching her arm. "Stay with me."

"Thank you." She rested her hand over Millie's. "But I can't." She removed Millie's hand from her arm. "You have to go. He won't be gone long."

"You can't stay here," Millie said.

"I don't have a choice."

"Yes, you do!" Millie stepped closer, but the young woman moved back inside. "You always have a choice."

"Go home." The young woman started to close the side door. "Get out of here before he comes back."

"I'm trying to save you!" She didn't mean to yell at her, but she did. "Why won't you let me save you?"

"You can't. You're just a kid." The young woman closed the side door and locked it.

Millie heard a car door shut. The terrified look on the young woman's face confirmed that she heard it too, and she pressed a finger against her broken lips. She disappeared into the house, leaving Millie alone in the backyard.

Millie waited until she heard the front door slam closed. She bolted to her house.

"Millie, is that you?"

"Yes. It's me."

"Where did you go?" Her father asked.

"Outside." Millie looked at her neighbor's house. She'd tried. That's all she could do. The young woman was right. She was a kid, but that young woman was married to a bully, a monster. She wasn't going to fight him.

Millie clenched her fists. Who the hell are those people to destroy others' lives? She thought of the bullies at her school, went upstairs, and turned her laptop on. She typed responses to their horrible posts and smiled. Millie would not allow anyone to break her apart again.

The rest of the day was quiet. Millie's father and mother barely looked at each other at dinner. Millie cleared the table and did the dishes again. She glanced up at the kitchen, but it was dark. No sign of life.

She spent the night watching television with her father until it was time for bed. Luckily, it wasn't the news. She called it a night and went to her bedroom. Lights flashed outside her window.

She looked outside. E.M.T.'s pulled a stretcher out of her neighbor's house with a body covered in a white sheet. Damn it. He killed her. He must have known Millie was at his house, trying to save her.

The two police officers from earlier stepped out of the house. In between them was the young woman. Her hands were cuffed together and coated in blood, his blood. She looked at Millie and smiled as the police officers guided her to the squad car.

She fought back. She saved her own life. But what will happen to her now? Will Millie ever see her again?

Millie took out her sketchpad and sketched the young woman being led outside by the police officers. Her face was still badly bruised. Her hands cuffed and red. Her right eye no longer shined with misery and pain. She smiled through her broken lips. She was finally free, free from him.

IS MOM OKAY?

*T*he world was in chaos, and we were talking about *Flowers for Algernon. It didn't end well for Charlie Gordon or the mouse. It won't end well for us. What was even more frustrating was that Mom was not answering her texts.*

Ryan sighed loudly as English class ended. He checked his cell phone. Why was she not answering him? It'd been weeks and nothing. He had let it go for a week, but even that was hard to do.

"Come on, Mom. It's been two weeks," Ryan texted. "Just text back one word. Okay. Just text me. Please."

Ryan sat in his chair and glanced at the computer on his desk. He was supposed to click for attendance. He had no patience for Social Studies. The world was falling apart outside, and nobody was paying attention to history. Instead of a nuclear bomb, it was a viral one. *Fuck Social Studies.* He clutched the cell phone in his hand and stormed out of his bedroom.

What if she was dead? He froze on the stairs, and the damn stairs creaked. "Shut up," he said to himself and listened for his father. He was still safe.

Outside the door to the study, Ryan heard his father saying something like, "Dynamics." His father didn't give a shit about what was happening outside his job, and he made it very clear he wasn't to be disturbed until five p.m. Ryan flipped the bird at the door and made his way into the kitchen.

At least his father made sure the kitchen was fully stocked. There was plenty of bottled water. Bread. Cheese. Eggs. Deli meat. What Ryan really wanted was a candy bar. The last time he had chocolate, he'd shared Sarah's candy bar during lunch before the lockdown. He should text Sarah.

What if she's gone, and all you want is a candy bar. He glanced at his cell phone.

"Why aren't you in class?"

Ryan thought of that show his father watched. Law & Order. His father stood behind him like Jerry Orbach with his arms crossed over his chest and a pissed look on his face. His father always looked pissed, and Ryan was tired of his attitude. *If only I could have stayed with Mom*, but that wasn't the agreement.

"I was hungry," Ryan said, returning his stare. "There's nothing to eat."

"You mean there's no junk food." His father sighed. "I got you cookies."

"I don't want cookies."

"Well, that's it. Take it or leave it."

Ryan grabbed a jar of peanut butter out of the fridge and closed the door.

"No jelly?"

"I hate jelly. Have you talked to Mom?" He watched his father take the white bread out of a kitchen drawer.

"Can you get the ham and cheese out of the fridge, please? We can talk about your mother later."

"She's not answering me." Ryan took the ham and cheese out of the fridge and watched his father make his sandwich. "It's been two weeks. She hasn't emailed me. No texts. No phone calls."

"She's fine," Ryan's father said.

"No, Dad. Something's wrong. I just have this feeling."

"Ryan, your mother's fine. Eat your peanut butter sandwich and get back to class."

"You're wrong! Just tell me you heard from her."

"I did." His father bit into his sandwich.

"When? When did you hear from her?"

His father tossed his sandwich onto a plate and took out a few napkins from the cabinet. He held one out, but Ryan did not move to take it. He placed the napkin near Ryan on a countertop.

"Look, it's Friday. You want to skip class today? Fine, but you will be in full attendance starting Monday. Got it?"

"Dad..."

"No. Your mother is fine. Stop worrying." His father carried his plate and napkin out of the kitchen.

"Come on, Mom. Answer me." He glanced from his phone to his sandwich. He pushed it away, then pulled it back. Continuing to peek at his cell, he forced himself to eat. "She's okay. She's okay," he said. *No, she's not.*

He left his half-finished lunch in the kitchen and walked into the family room. He texted Sarah. They were best friends. He actually wanted to be more than friends, but she had a crush on some guy in the eighth grade. The guy was a jerk. *Didn't Sarah realize that?*

"Hi, Ryan," she texted. "Sorry it took so long. It's been pretty scary over here. My brother got sick. My parents quarantined me to my bedroom. Haven't seen my brother in weeks. My parents seem fine. Don't know what's going on."

"I'm sorry," Ryan texted back. *I love you, Sarah.* "I'm sorry," he texted again.

"Your mother is essential. Right?"

"She's an Administrative Secretary. She was told that she's essential."

"Heard from her?"

Ryan stared at Sarah's words. *Heard from her? No. I think she's dead, but she's not. I hope she's not.* Tears filled his eyes, and he quickly wiped them away. "No," he texted.

"I would be worried."

"I have to go. Please, stay safe. I hope you and your family are okay."

"Same. Text me later."

"I will." Ryan brushed more tears away. "Fuck this," he said and returned to the kitchen.

No matter the circumstances, Ryan was told not to call his mother at work. He was only to contact her by her cell phone and text. This was different. This was a crisis. He walked over to the phone on the wall. He would keep it quick. He just needed to know she was okay.

"Operator," an older woman said. "What extension?"

"Operator? This is not a direct line anymore?"

"All calls are being routed through the call service, sir. Who are you trying to reach?"

"Amanda. Amanda Quinzel."

"One moment, please." A long pause followed. "I'm sorry. There is no extension for her. I believe she is inside."

"Inside?"

"Inside the compound."

No. No! "No, you're wrong."

"Who's calling for her?"

Ryan hung up the phone. *Inside? Inside the compound?* That meant she was exposed or would be exposed. Was that why she wasn't answering him? *She's sick, you idiot. She's probably dead.*

"No, she's not," he yelled into the kitchen.

A knock came from the front door. Maybe his mom lost her cell phone. Maybe she couldn't text him. Maybe he was keeping her waiting.

"Mom!" Ryan threw open the door to see a postal worker standing outside.

"Hello. Not your mother. Sorry." The postal worker placed a small box on the porch. "Leave this on the porch until tomorrow. If you bring it inside now, use gloves, and wash your hands."

"Who's it for?"

"Ryan Quinzel. It's from an Amanda Quinzel." Ryan snatched the box and stared at the label. "You need to wash your hands."

"This was sent two weeks ago," he said.

"I'm sorry. We're having issues with everything. Wash your hands." She stepped away.

"Wait. What's it like in Rockland?"

"It's a hot spot."

"Hot spot," Ryan repeated and took the box inside, placing it on the floor. He ran to the downstairs bathroom and washed his hands for twenty seconds with hot water and soap, then pushed the front door shut. In the kitchen, he grabbed a pair of scissors to cut the top of the box open. Inside was a stack of DC Comic Books and two candy bars.

Ryan washed his hands again. He washed the scissors and returned them to the kitchen drawer. Carefully, he reached inside the box and took out the comic books and candy bars. A small card slipped out and fell to the floor.

"Dear Ryan," the card said. "I will always be close. Love, Mom."

His mother's words sliced through him. He tore up the stairs, tears pouring down his face, and dropped the comic books and chocolate onto his bed. He threw his pillow over the candy bars, sat in his chair with his back away from the desk, and allowed himself to cry.

"Ryan?" His father opened the bedroom door. Ryan watched him glance over at the bed. "See? Your mother is just fine."

"She sent them two weeks ago."

"Okay." He watched Ryan wipe away his tears. "Come on. Let's go."

"Where?"

"Downstairs to the kitchen. You can get yourself a glass of water while I call your mother."

"What about your job?"

"Don't be a smartass." Ryan's father patted him on the head as they walked down the stairs.

Ryan got himself a glass of water.

"Actually, I'm going to call Becky." His father picked up the kitchen phone and dialed a number.

Becky was the next-door neighbor and a good friend of Ryan's mother. Ryan could tell she was calling his father some choice words, but he took it.

"I understand you haven't seen her lately. Ryan is very worried, and so am I. Yes, I am worried about her. It's been too long. Please, Becky. Check on her and call me back. Thank you." He hung up the phone.

"Now, what?"

"Now, we wait. Go eat your candy bar." His father smiled. "I know your mother."

Ryan stepped away but then looked at his father. "Do you still love her?"

"It's complicated, Ryan."

"What if Becky doesn't call back?"

"She will. Go on. Go upstairs and read your comic books."

He saw his father look at the phone. *He's worried. Very worried.* He wanted to say something but left the kitchen.

Ryan sat on his bed and flipped through the comic books. He couldn't bring himself to read them, but he ate a candy bar and placed the other in his desk drawer.

Hours dragged by. He didn't play on his computer. He sat on the bed, waited, and checked his cell. It was finally time for dinner, and still no phone call.

"I'm making frozen pizza," Ryan's father said. "It should be ready in ten minutes. Want to set the table?"

Ryan didn't feel like it, but he set the table, then sat in a chair and waited. *I'm tired of waiting!* He glanced at the phone. *Who uses a fucking landline anyway?* Maybe Becky wasn't reliable after all. His father brought him a slice, and he quietly ate it.

The phone rang, and they jumped. Ryan's father answered the phone. He nodded at Ryan.

"Thank God," Ryan said. "She's okay. Mom's okay."

His father turned and faced the wall.

"Yes, I understand. Please, let me know. Thank you, Becky." He hung up and rested his hand on the phone.

Dad?" His father didn't answer him. "Dad?"

His father lowered his hand and finally looked at Ryan, tears shining in his eyes. "She has the virus."

"Now, Ryan. You be good to your father. Don't give him a hard time." Ryan saw his mother standing by the front door. It was two weeks ago. "I'll be back soon. I love you. Be good," she said.

"I love you, Mom," Ryan said.

WORKING EIGHT TO FIVE ON THE SUPPLY LINE

Seven-thirty a.m. My car was parked in its slot. The machines raced over and sprayed the car like it was in a car wash. I waited until they were done, then exited the car. I followed the small, flashing red path to the containment doors. Inside the doors, I was sprayed. Decontaminated. I held my breath, pressing my lips tight against the taste of the purifier. That taste took forever to leave my mouth. Finally, the electronic doors opened, and I stepped into the building.

Following along another red path, I found myself limping to my booth. My left leg didn't always bother me, but it seemed to a lot these days. I bent down to rub my leg. As I did, I watched the others arrive. We were not allowed to speak. We were not allowed to touch. Social distancing felt like isolation. Another set of doors opened, and I stepped inside. The doors banged shut behind me.

At least, my chair was comfortable. I strapped in and snapped the computer console on. I hated the gloves, so constricting, and the wires bit into my skin. As the monitor glowed green, I picked up the helmet. It felt like a bowling ball in my hands, at least six pounds, and it was tight around my head.

Darkness faded into the cabin. The truck's engine revved up. Blue skies with soft, white clouds was seen outside the windshield. How I missed that view, and my hands tightened around the wheel. I reached down and shifted gears. As I did, a schedule flashed across the dashboard—New York City. First stop. Hopefully, not the last. The city was in dire need of supplies but so was everywhere else.

No traffic. No cars on the road. Just trucks.

"Calling Deckard. Calling Deckard. You out there? Please, come in."

"That you, Devil Candy?" I asked.

"That's me, honey. How are you this fine morning?"

"Alive." I still tasted that damn decontaminant. "Could use a cup of coffee right about now."

"I miss coffee," she said. "I don't remember my last cup. Withdrawal's a bitch." She laughed.

I laughed too. "Lucky for me, I still have some cigarettes."

"You smoke in there, and they'll fire your ass."

"Nah. I save my cigs for special occasions."

"Oh, yeah? Like what?" She asked. "After you kill a Blade Runner?"

"Replicant."

"What?"

"I can't believe you never saw Blade Runner."

"The one with Ryan Gosling. Yeah, I saw that one."

"The original one." I glanced at the CB radio, but I knew we were talking through our helmets. "I save my cigarettes for my wife and son's birthday." She didn't answer me. "So, Devil, where ya headed?"

"New Mexico. You?"

"New York City."

"What a shithole. They let that city fall apart."

"A lot of cities fell apart. Look who's running the country."

"Too early for politics, Deckard. Have you heard from West Davies?"

"No. It's been radio silent. I'm a little concerned."

"Well, you didn't hear it from me, but I heard he got a little gun happy."

"Gun happy? As in protecting his family with a gun?"

"No. As in doing something stupid, like breaking into his neighbor's house to raid their supplies. What did he think? That he would rob them and go to work like nothing happened? Stupid."

"Some people are stupid, but at least the authorities are still doing their jobs."

"As best as they can. It's amazing that these roads are so empty."

I stared out at the blue skies with the soft, white clouds. "Everyone's inside," I said.

"Or they're dead."

The taste of decontaminant was finally gone. I cleared my throat, glancing outside again. The trees were starting to change color. Was it fall already? Where did the time go? Where did my life go?

The deliveries served a purpose to me. They got me out of the house, and in return, I was taken care of. The company provided me with food, clothes, and their doctors, but their doctors were even lost like me. None of us were ready for what happened. A lot of people died.

"Why did West Davies get so greedy?" I meant to keep this inside, but I said it out loud.

"He didn't like what the company was giving him. Yes, he got greedy. And he got dead."

"He's dead?"

"He got sick shortly after. Maybe, from being in a cell with others. I don't know. Fucking idiot. I'm sorry, Deckard. I shouldn't be bothering you. We are at work after all."

"It's okay, Devil. It's good to hear your voice. Makes me remember that I'm still alive. We're still alive."

"Well, at least you have a family to go home to. I'll catch you later. Stay safe. Keep well."

"Stay safe. Keep well."

The cab turned quiet. I liked driving in the quiet, feeling the steering wheel in my hands, my feet against the pedals. I would have enjoyed life on the road, but in another life. Not this one.

There was a military outpost outside of New York City. The guards waved me through without a second thought. That was the last human existence I saw before I pulled into my destination.

"Lunch Time." The console ripped me back to reality. I took off the helmet as a little machine darted into the booth, spitting out a bottle of water and crackers wrapped in plastic. Some lunch, but I didn't complain. I didn't say thank you either. I just ate, drank, and itched to get back out there. Hit the road, even if I was really stuck in here, a square, metal cube.

Next stop, L.A. The truck left the station, and I headed in that direction. The blue skies were still there, but the soft, white clouds were gone. I was still grateful to be outside, if you could call this, outside. I just didn't want to go home. I was doing a service—doing good. The supply line needed to run, and those that were left needed to survive.

We survived because some brainiac in his basement came up with merging drone technology with V.R. Their idea is holding the human race together, otherwise we would all huddle inside waiting to die or do something stupid like West Davies. How did he get sick, but I didn't want to know.

"Deckard. You there?"

"Hello, Devil Candy. How many runs did you do today?"

"Four. You?"

"Just three."

"Supply loads are getting smaller."

"Nah. The manufacturers just need more time."

"I hope you're right, for all our sakes. Plans tonight?"

"Just going home. You?"

"The same. Speak to you tomorrow?"

"I hope so. You be safe out there."

"You too. Take care of your family and get some rest. Later."

"Later." I pulled off the helmet and drew in a breath. I didn't taste air. I tasted manufactured air conditioning. What did air taste like now?

When I got outside, I tried to hold my breath, move fast, and jump into my car. In the car, I could breathe, but when I got home, it would be the same thing. Try not to breathe in the air. It was so hard, but I did it.

The front door shut behind me as I raced inside and grabbed a can of decontaminant spray. I sprayed myself, waited a few moments, and breathed. I went upstairs and jumped into a hot shower, scrubbing every part of my body.

I stepped out of the shower and slid on a light, company issued pajama suit. It reminded me of those onesies a child would wear. I walked back downstairs, not bothering to turn on the lights.

In the kitchen, I cracked open a can of tuna fish and another bottle of water and ate, staring at the wall. I reached under the table for my cigarettes. Three left. I took one, then grabbed a lighter out of the drawer.

I sat in the living room, again not bothering to turn on any lights or the television. Entertainment was dead. A lot of things were. I should hit the hay. The next day was another workday, and I prayed the manufacturers were still producing supplies, that the supply lines would continue to run. *Please, God, tell me that this isn't how it ends.*

I paused by the fireplace, the cigarette burning red in the darkness. My hand graced the picture of my wife and son. "Happy birthday, son." I started to cry. "If only you both..." I crushed the cigarette against the brick and wiped my tears away.

I saved lives. I knew I did, but it would never make up for losing them. Even if we find a way to survive, the world would never be the same again. None of us would be the same again. I can't stay here in this house without them. I would go insane. Saving lives had to be enough, or at least, I would keep telling myself that. *But what if we don't survive?* No, people were counting on me, and I would keep delivering until I got sick. Then, someone else would step in and take my eight to five job and keep the supply line running. If anyone was left.

The supply line had to keep running.

I WANT TO GO HOME

I *miss the busy streets. The sound of traffic. The chime of the door opening and closing. The voices of people. The echo of laughter. A gentle touch. A loving look, sometimes chased with a hint of sadness.*

They're all gone.

The streets had been empty for a long time. Sometimes, a car passed by, but it didn't stop. They're afraid to stop. They run the red light, then nothing but quiet until another car raced by as if chased by the need to get to where they were going. The door to this place remained shut.

He used to come twice a day, his face and hands covered. In the beginning, he would still give me a pat on the head, lower his mask, and smile. That quickly changed. He made sure we had food and water and clean litter boxes, but then he would leave, almost as if he was afraid to stay with us. The door shut and locked behind him. I don't remember what the air felt like except for a biting cold rush.

I miss the rain. I don't miss the streets. He rescued me, but he left me here, without him.

The others don't seem to mind. They stretched out in the sun. They chased their tails. They played with the merchandise. One spent the morning chewing on their nails. The oldest cat stayed in his bed on a shelf near the register. He hadn't moved in days.

Then, he returned. He stood in front of that bed with the oldest cat for a long time. When he glanced my way, tears ran down his face and under his mask. *My friend was gone.*

I didn't think things could get any worse. I was wrong.

A week went by. He had stopped coming in. We ran out of food. We ran out of water. There was a sink in the backroom, and we were lucky he left the door open. We took turns drinking out of the sink and the toilet bowl. The litter boxes filled up. We even used the bathroom floor.

We waited. We waited a long time. I did not think he was coming back.

Another week went by. He returned, but he was thinner, his eyes empty. He cleaned out the litter boxes. He picked up the empty food and water dishes. He didn't refill them. He put them away. He moved over to the store door and propped it open. One by one, he pushed us outside. I was the last one to go.

I met his gaze, and he stared at me like he didn't know me. But he did. He does, but he closed the door and kept it shut. A moment later, he placed a For Sale Sign in the window and turned away.

My friends moved on, but I didn't.

I want to go home. This is where I belong, but there is no more home to go back to. Only the streets.

AT THE ORANGE LIGHT

The lights were off in the gentle white room. Two chairs sat facing the traffic light across the street. The traffic light flashed red, then orange. It turned green.

Valerie sat in a chair, the other one was empty. "Red or Green?" She didn't like the quiet. Ben was getting weaker, and she knew what that meant. But he had to hold on. "Red or green?" she asked again.

"Val, I don't want to play anymore." Ben stood in front of her and looked at the empty chair. "We've talked for weeks. Nothing's changed." Sadness clung to his voice. "There is nothing left to say."

"Everything's changed, Ben." Valerie looked out the window, struggling to hold the tears back. "Everyone's changed." She pulled at her soft, white gown.

"Then why talk about the past?" Ben reached around the back, feeling the knot on his gown. "Why talk about yesterday?" He sat down in the chair.

"Because there's no today." Valerie's tears escaped, and she wiped them aside. She forced a smile and touched his hand. "Come on. In the beginning, we didn't say a word to each other. We just sat here in silence and watched the traffic light outside. Then, you said you always liked green, so on the green, you would talk about your life. On the red, I talk about mine."

"I'm tired." Ben patted her hand. "I'm very tired." He pulled his hand away, but Valerie grabbed hold of it. "I think it's time."

"So, what? That's it? You're going to leave me here all alone?" Her grip tightened. "What about your wife?"

"I don't even know if she is alive."

"Your kids?"

"I pray they and my grandchildren are safe. I hope they are not fools like the ones that the nurses and doctors talk about."

"You've been married to your wife for how long?"

"Almost fifty years."

"And how many kids?"

"Two, Val. Grown up with grandchildren."

"So, don't you want to see them again?"

"Do you think that I don't?" Anger. That was good. When he was angry, he looked more alive. "My granddaughter is turning three tomorrow. She is not going to remember me. The only thing she'll have to know that I existed are pictures and stories. That kills me." He flinched with those words. "No one was ready for this." He glanced at the traffic light. "Red."

"None of us were ready." Valerie let go of his hand. "I'm not even forty yet, and I'm not married. I just have my parents, and last year, I was told I couldn't have kids." She noted Ben's surprise, and then his expression changed to pity. "Please, don't pity me."

"Did you want kids?" Now, he touched her hand.

"Not at first. Then, I thought about it and decided it was for the best. My life was … is not the most stable. What kind of mother would I be? Now, I wish I had at least one child but look at the world today. How could I do that to her?"

"Her?"

Valerie gazed past the door and out into the hallway. "I would have liked a daughter."

"If it was a boy?"

Valerie watched a nurse walk by. "I guess it wouldn't matter. Doesn't matter." She looked at Ben. "It is what it is." The traffic light flipped to green. "Your turn."

"I don't dream anymore." Ben stood up from his chair. "They say that when you have the virus, you have vivid dreams. I did in the beginning, but this week, nothing. I feel nothing." He looked at her, but it felt like he was looking through her. "I feel numb. My mind is quiet, so is my heart."

Valerie brushed another tear aside. Red. "I lived with Mason for two years. He never wanted kids. He always asked if I took precautions. Precautions. The more I think about Mason, the more I realize he was an ass, who controlled me. I hope he gets sick. I hope he dies."

"Valerie! Don't say that."

"He never loved me. All the guys that I've been with. None of them ever loved me. I don't know what love is. Maybe, if I could have adopted a kid, that would change, but I'm sick. We're sick, and we've been stuck in this damn room for too long." Valerie cried. "Maybe we're never leaving here."

Ben leaned over and embraced her. He felt cold, like he was already gone. His grip tightened. She hugged him back and cried against his chest. Maybe her cries would touch his heart, bring him back.

"I love you," Ben whispered into her ear.

She leaned back and wiped her tears aside. "You don't even know me."

"I know you. If not for playing Red or Green, I would have been lost. I would have already been gone." He moved back into his seat, and a look she did not like passed over his face. "You can't hold on to me, Val." He looked at her, and she flinched. "I'm slipping away."

"Ben!" She grabbed hold of his arm. "Stay! Please. For me."

"I'm amazed that I awoke this morning, if it is morning. There's no clock in here. Just machines. I'm sorry." His stare cut through her. "You heard the news. Before you came here. So many of us are gone, and for what? Why? Why did this have to happen to us?"

"I don't know." She looked down at her hand. It was still on his arm. "I'm sorry."

"It's not your fault."

"It's not your fault either, Ben. Life happens, and that's it. We deal with it, and we hope to survive."

"Until it breaks us down again." Ben rested his hand over hers. He glanced out the window. "Green. Val, I need you to do me a favor."

"Ben, don't."

"Please. I need you to find my wife. Tell her that my last thoughts were of her."

"Ben, please. Please, don't ask that of me."

"Tell her I know that she couldn't visit me here. They wouldn't let her in, but I don't blame her for that. It's not her fault, and I love her. I love my children, my grandchildren." He watched Valerie cry and slowly nod. "Thank you. Thank you for being my friend."

"I'll tell her." Valerie wiped her eyes, but the tears kept coming. "Thank you, Ben. Thank you for being my friend."

"I'm sure you will return home soon."

Valerie glanced out the window. The traffic light flashed orange. When she looked back at Ben, he was gone.

Footsteps hurried into the room. "Someone, call the doctor!"

Valerie tried to steady herself and watched the traffic light turn from red to green and green to red. She would have to get used to being alone, but she wouldn't forget Ben. She would find his wife. She would tell her how much Ben loved her and his children and grandchildren.

If only someone had loved her that much.

"He's alive!" A doctor turned to a nurse standing nearby. "We need to get him off the ventilator. Now!"

"What about the other patient, doctor? How is she doing?"

"I'm sorry." The doctor shook his head and glanced at the two chairs by the window, but he didn't see Valerie.

Valerie closed her eyes. "Red or Green?" She asked herself. "Red."

The sound of a flatline filled the room.

A SILVER LINING ACROSS THE DARK SKIES

He looked at me in the same way the other drivers that drove away from me, with distrust. It seemed he didn't want to be bothered, but something made him pause. Was it the rain falling hard on me? Did I remind him of someone he lost, or was it my large belly? Whatever it was, it made him look twice. There was something in his eyes. Something I had not seen in a long time. Compassion.

"Get in before you get soaked," he snapped, opening the passenger door of his semi-trailer truck. "Come on, already. I have a schedule to keep." I heard the regret in his voice, and I didn't move. "Are you coming?"

I picked up my green duffel bag. Well, it was my brother's. Now it was mine. His duffel bag was the only thing I had left of home. I struggled to get into the truck. He helped me up into the seat, but he was hesitant. People were still afraid to touch each other. I finally got into my seat, and he slammed the door shut.

There was a silver chain hanging around the rearview mirror. Attached to it was a small, black cross. I reached for it but then quickly pulled my hand back.

"Someone in your condition should not be out in this weather," he said. "And should not be hitching rides." He revved up the engine. "What would your parents think?"

"They're dead."

He looked at me for a long moment. Then, he led the Semi-trailer truck out of the parking lot and onto the road.

For the next hour, I stared out the passenger-side window. It was getting brighter outside, and the sun tried to shine its light through the trees. Nothing but dirt, trees, and the road, and I felt his eyes moving from the windshield over to my belly.

"Rain stopped," he said.

"I know," I answered.

"How far am I taking you?"

"As far as you can." I avoided his gaze, and he looked at my belly again.

"We have a game on the road," he said. "How many funeral processions do you see in a day?"

"That's morbid."

"No one said it was a fun game." He turned on the windshield wipers, wiping away the last of the rain. He glanced over at me. "I'm Hal."

"Rain."

"Fine. Don't tell me your real name."

"That is my real name," I said. "I have a brother called Thunder. My other brother is Hail with an I."

"Were your parents hippies?" He was surprised by my laugh, but my laugh quickly faded away. "Did your brothers make it?"

"Yes, my brothers did."

"Why aren't you with them?" He glanced at my stomach. "Did the father make it?"

"I don't know. I don't know anything." I looked at one finger and picked at the skin. I stopped and folded my hands together. "It's just me now."

"Does the father even know?" He continued to drive, looking out at the road.

I looked at him, and he flinched at my stare. "Things weren't good in my town before the virus."

"What town?" Hal asked.

"Lindenhurst." I looked out the window, knowing what was coming next.

"Lindenhurst. Why is that town so familiar?"

"There was a shooting there last October. At the school. Nine kids and one teacher dead. The shooter should have been killed, but he was only wounded. I hope he's dead from the virus."

I closed my eyes. I remembered that it was a regular morning. The substitute teacher was lecturing me about cheating on the math test. It was just a stupid test. It wasn't like I needed to know algebra.

Pop. I covered my ears, ignoring Hal's stare. *Pop.* I had stepped out into the hallway, and there he was, pointing his gun at me. *Pop*, and I was knocked to the floor.

I heard the shooter walk away, his footsteps fading with each breath I took. I remained lying still until I was sure he was gone, then looked at the substitute teacher lying on top of me. Was he still alive? I struggled to crawl out from beneath him. My clothes were soaked in his blood. I pushed my hands against the hole in his stomach. I didn't think he was going to make it. We stayed like that until rescue finally came.

My parents argued with me about visiting him at the hospital after school. I was a senior and had to focus on my grades. They didn't understand that he saved my life. I owed him, so I ignored my parents and visited him at the hospital.

During one visit, he told me that he was divorced. His wife got custody of his kids. They didn't live in the town, and she wasn't bringing his kids to see him. He was alone, and he needed someone. He needed me.

"I'm sorry," Hal said. "It's a rough patch."

"What is?" I shook the memories away but could still feel them stirring in my mind.

"The shooting, and then the virus."

"Things happen." I glanced at Hal and then closed my eyes.

We weren't supposed to fall for one another. I felt a tear slide down my face. "You were just supposed to take care of him," I whispered to myself.

"What?" Hal asked.

"Nothing," I said, wiping a tear aside.

I visited him at his house and took care of him. That was supposed to be the extent of it. I was leaving late one night when he took my hand in his and kissed me. I kissed him back.

"Don't you want to go back home?"

"I have no home." I still felt his kiss on my lips.

I'd tried to keep the pregnancy a secret. For a while, it worked. Until after the holidays. My mother knew. I don't know how she knew, but it was a shitstorm in January.

My parents were ready to press charges. I wasn't even eighteen yet. I begged them not to, and I thought I convinced them. But the police came to my school and arrested him. He was all over the news, and so was I.

The trial was set for February. By then, I was showing. I was struggling through school. My parents told me not to drop out, but they didn't understand what it was like there. I was treated terribly by the students and the teachers. It was hell, and then I had to testify in court.

I was condemning the man that saved my life. When I didn't think it could get any worse, the virus came. It got a lot worse.

During my preparation, the lawyer started to cough. It wasn't a regular cough, and he couldn't stop. My father grabbed me and pulled me away from the lawyer. He knew the lawyer had the virus. He coughed on my father, and that was the beginning of the end. If they had just fucking listened to me, then maybe my parents would still be alive today.

"You okay?" Hal asked.

I didn't realize I was crying more. I crossed my arms over my chest, trying to will myself to stop. The tears fell, but luckily for me, I was a quiet crier, not one of those loud sobbers. "Funeral procession," I said.

"What?" Hal looked at the road. "You get the first point," he said. "You want some air? I could roll down the window."

"I don't want to smell the dead." I touched the surgical mask on my face. Sometimes, I forgot it was there. I realized that Hal was wearing one too. "What's today's date? I can never keep track of the days."

"May 1st. My son always looked forward to Memorial Day. The parade. The barbecue." Hal's voice shook, and a tear escaped down his face. "Nothing's the same anymore." He wiped his tear away.

"Did he make it?"

"He did. My wife didn't." Hal focused on the road in front of him.

"I'm sorry."

"Thank you." He looked at me. "I'm sorry about your parents. Why aren't your brothers there for you? Aren't you almost due?"

"Almost," I replied. I couldn't tell him the second part. "Where is your son?"

"With my sister." He glanced at the radio. It looked like someone took a hammer to it, maybe a fist. "I broke the radio. I couldn't take it. So much death. So much bullshit. Doesn't matter now."

"Doesn't it?" I asked.

"No. You either died from the virus, or you survived it. It's amazing that you survived with your condition."

That was the second part. I thought it was a miracle. My family didn't. We lost my father first. My mother followed shortly afterward. Both of my brothers got sick. One not so bad, but Hail got it worse. We didn't think he would live, but he did. My brothers expected me to get sick. They worried about the baby, but we were both fine. They didn't understand and blamed me for our parents. If I was never pregnant, then our parents would still be alive. I got them all exposed. My brothers couldn't forgive me for that.

"Fuck," Hal said. "Check point."

A black sign flashed yellow letters. Virus Check Point. Why were they still checking? I placed my hand over my belly. "Shit," I said.

"You okay?"

"I'm fine."

"The baby?"

"Fine."

"Then, what? What's wrong?" Hal looked at me and then at my belly.

"I have to tell you something."

"I'm the father?" I could tell that he smiled at my laugh. "You needed that."

"I did. Hal, I'm immune to the virus."

"What? That's not possible. No one is immune to the virus."

"I am."

"You're wrong, Rain."

That was the first time he had said my name. "I'm not wrong. The virus tore through my family. I lost my parents. I almost lost one of my brothers, but I didn't get the virus."

"Haven't you seen a doctor?"

"Not since March," I said. "Why are they checking anyway?"

"I don't know, but I wonder if others are immune like you. Maybe, that's why they are checking. Would that be such a bad thing?" He glanced at me and then back at the road.

I placed a hand over my belly. "Yes, it would be," I said.

"Well, it's just a wand that they swipe across your forehead. You've been exposed to the virus, so it should turn green. There shouldn't be an issue," but Hal didn't even sound convinced.

"Can we go around it?"

"No, we can't. It'll be okay." He reached over and gingerly touched my hand. "Do you know what you are having?"

"No," I said. "It doesn't matter."

He pulled his hand away. "Don't you have anyone, anyone at all?"

"No. It's fine, Hal." The baby kicked. It was a hard kick, and I flinched. I flinched again as I saw people in hazmat suits wave for us to slow down and stop.

One of the people in hazmat suits gestured for Hal to exit the truck. He left his door open, and I watched them swipe that wand across his forehead. It turned green.

Hal walked around the truck and opened my door. He helped me out of my seat, and I saw the surprise on some of the people's faces. He was touching me.

Another person in a hazmat suit waved the wand across my forehead. It turned red. Again, everyone looked surprised.

"Maybe it's broken," Hal said.

"No. It works," a man in the hazmat suit replied. "She's immune, and I bet so is the baby." He placed a hand over my belly. "We could use them both."

A truck blasted through the check point. It must have been carrying something contaminated or contraband. The men in hazmat suits started yelling at each other. They stepped away except for two. They grabbed hold of me and gestured for Hal to return to his Semi-trailer truck.

"I'm going to call this in," one man in a hazmat suit said. "Hold her. She can't get away."

I looked down at my belly. It was over. I had failed to protect myself and my baby.

The man holding me was knocked over. It was Hal, and he hurried me over to his truck.

"Get in!"

Hal wasted no time getting me into the passenger's seat. He kicked the engine into gear and slammed on the gas. He floored it past the other truck now pulled over and the men in hazmat suits.

A long moment passed before Hal said, "You weren't kidding about being immune."

"No," I said. "I wasn't."

"How are you immune?"

"I don't know." What if I was immune because of him, the substitute teacher? Did he save my life twice? I realized that I was sweating, but I felt cold. "All I know is that I'm alive, and so is my baby. I don't want them coming for us. I don't want them to take my baby away from me." My baby kicked me. Hard.

"That won't happen," Hal said.

"They probably have your license plate."

"Look, I know someone. He doesn't live too far from here, and he's a good man. He'll take care of you and the baby."

"And those people back there?"

"They won't find you, Rain. I won't tell them anything." He took my hand in his and looked at it. It must have been a long time since he held someone's hand. "Let me help you and the baby. Please."

"Okay," I said. "Let's go."

Hal checked the rearview mirror as he continued to drive. I wrapped my arms around my belly as best as I could. What kind of world was I bringing this child into? Would they be safe? Nothing was normal anymore.

Too many people were afraid, and the news would get out about me. Again. Another controversy, but I trusted Hal. He kept me safe, and if he trusted this man, then I trusted him too.

I don't know what kind of future awaited me. I used to imagine all kinds, but then the shooting happened. Then, the virus. My future scared me, but maybe it's not all lost. Maybe there's a silver lining across the dark skies, and my baby kicked inside me.

THE YARD

Something dark had brought them here. Maybe they understood what they had done. Some never would. They stood together, enjoying the summer air. *Do they hear the birds sing as they nest in the windows of their buildings? Do they listen to the traffic coming from a world outside the barbed wire fence? Do they know the pandemic raging and why they all have to wear a mask?*

I envied their realities. Multiple versions of real life. If I could escape, I would, but I'm a prisoner too. Many men have been caught on the barbed wire, their blood staining metal. Exposure to the staff even before the pandemic. The virus had quietly slid inside. It was here, walking among them. They were better off not knowing. If they did, they would be afraid. They would be afraid of us. We were the ones that let it in.

A staff member hurried across the yard, careful to keep their distance. It was not in respect for social distancing. It was out of fear. They touched their mask with their gloves, making sure it was still in place. Now the mask was contaminated. *Would they still wear their mask or change it once inside the building? Did it matter? We're all infected.*

Two male staff passed by, their masks tucked under their chins. They walked close, laughing about old times. They think it's over, but every word out of their mouth was a viral bombardment, unseen and possibly deadly. *Did they even think about it? Did they care? Would they care later when the virus found them?* The clang of the gate slammed shut as they left for lunch.

It was almost time to go back inside. Time. I never thought about it, but I wasted it plenty. I won't get time back. I don't know how much I have left. *How much time do they have left?* If they could spend eternity out here in the yard, they would. We all would, but the world doesn't work like that. It's too wound up, ticking to its end, and we are ticking with it. There is no escape. I want to live my life beyond these pale, concrete walls. *But I'm a prisoner too.*

They're better off not knowing, struggling to keep their demons inside. There was evil in this world, whether we wanted to believe it or not. Sometimes, it leads here. Sometimes, it stays outside. Either way, those like me can't ignore it, but we do. Well, I did. *Not anymore.* It's time to go back inside.

EVEN DOWNPOURS WILL PASS

Hard rain fell on Everwood Lane. Raindrops raced each other into oblivion and played cars like drums. A stray cat looked like a wet mop, and only the rain held conversation, yet it failed to drown out the news.

Roble sat on the couch, watching the rain fall, sighing with each drop. His ears begged for more roar, anything just to silence the news. He stared into the gray. That was his world. Gray and chaos. So much chaos, haunted with so much death. No room for life. But then he saw a little girl staring out her family room window at him.

Roble raised his hand. The little girl replied, then wiped her eyes. She could not have been more than ten. He was twice that age. Her sadness mirrored the rain, the gray, and it cut right through him.

Lightning flashed, and he bolted from the couch. He returned but didn't see the little girl. He took a felt pen and drew a grid on the family room window, not caring if his parents had another meltdown. When he looked up, the little girl was there but ran away. She returned with a marker and drew on her window.

Roble pointed at the upper right corner. She made an X with her fingers. Roble drew an X and so did she. The little girl pointed at the lower left space, and Roble made an O shape with his hand. She drew an O. He pointed at the middle, and the little girl made another X. She gestured to the upper left, and Roble signed with an O. In the end, he lost, but the little girl won.

Roble mirrored the little girl's smile, then wiped away their game with a wet and dry paper towel. He could spend the rest of the time watching the rain fall with her, but her smile didn't last. Her tears were as strong as the rain.

He grabbed more markers from the kitchen drawer, returned to the family room, and looked out the window. The little girl was frantically scrubbing at the glass, not paying attention to Roble.

On the window, he wrote, "I'm Sorry" in pink and green, followed by a colored in red heart.

The little girl stared at Roble and wiped her eyes. She read his words, "I'm Sorry" and smiled. Her gaze settled on the heart. She made a hug gesture, not realizing that her mother was standing behind her. Her mother at first looked furious, but then she took the marker from the little girl and drew a bigger heart across the window.

WHAT DO WE DREAM IN BETWEEN

Sunlight flooded the catering hall. Little, red rose petals decorated the floor. Baskets of white flowers rested against the walls. Tables were set with white and gold plates over white linen tablecloths. Name cards waited by glasses filled with ice water. A small altar of entwined red and white flowers stood at the end of the aisle. The bride sat in her gown on the steps leading into the room. She was the only one there.

"I don't understand," she said. "I was married. The wedding happened. It happened, so where is everyone? Where is my husband?"

She remembered getting married. Everyone was there. The groom was there. It was a beautiful service, and she and her husband ran outside to their waiting limo. But the memory did not feel real. She kept coming back here to this catering hall, sitting on the steps leading into the room.

"I don't get it." She leaned down into her white bridal dress and cried. "Where is everyone? Where is my husband?"

"They're not here." Her father stood behind her dressed in a black and white tuxedo. "It's just you and me." He sat beside her. His hand moved over hers.

"But they were here. They should be here. Why aren't they here? Why doesn't this feel real?"

"Look, we don't have much time." His hand tightened over hers.

"Everything was supposed to be perfect. Today was my day."

"Yes, honey." Her father wiped away her tears. "Today was supposed to be your day."

"Supposed to be? I did everything right, Dad. I made sure of it." She felt faint as if she were slipping away, and she clung to her father's hand. "I got... Sick."

Her father turned away, but his hand never left hers. "Yes, you did." He looked at her, and the sadness in his eyes broke her heart. "I'm sorry, but it's over."

"Dad?" She held her father's gaze, watching the tears pour down his face. "No. No!" She pulled her hand away and wiped her tears aside. "It can't end like this. I did everything right, and I didn't even get to... To marry him." She stood up and looked at her white bridal dress. "Why am I here? Why, Dad?"

"You're in between," her father said in a low voice.

"What does that mean?" Her father didn't answer her. She stepped away from him and looked around the catering hall. "I'm in the hospital." For a moment, her dress flickered into a hospital gown. "I'm dead," she said.

"No, you're not dead." Her father wiped his tears away and looked at her. "Not yet."

"Why are you here?" She looked at her father and stepped back. "Are you really my father?"

A dark shadow fell over her father but then quickly faded away. "Yes, I'm really your father." He stood up and walked toward her. "I can't explain how. But I am here. For you." He reached for her, but she stepped back.

"No. This is wrong. I am dead, but I'm still wearing heels?" She kicked off her white shoes. "What's that?" The sun disappeared, and the room fell into shadow. Voices filled the space around her. "Who's talking?"

"The doctor," her father said. "He's talking to the nurse. They're getting ready."

"No! Please. Please, Dad, don't let them pull the plug. I'm not dead." She grabbed hold of her father. "I'm here. I'm right here!"

"I know." Her father hugged her. "And I'm sitting right beside your bed, whether they want me there or not, and I'm holding your hand."

She looked at her father. "This isn't fair." She looked away. "None of this is fair."

"I didn't want you to be alone." Her father touched her face. "That's why I'm here."

"I wanted you to see me like this on my wedding day. Not like this."

"I know." Her father's voice shook.

She pushed her tears aside. "There is something that you can do for me before ..."

"Anything," her father said.

"Walk me down the aisle. Please."

Her father smiled, and she smiled with him. He wrapped his arm around hers, more tears poured down his face, and she cried with him. He led her down the aisle and stopped before the altar of red and white flowers. He plucked one of each from the altar and placed them in her hands.

"I love you," her father said.

"I love you too." She felt his kiss on her cheek and faded away.

RED BIRDS SING OF YESTERDAY

R ed birds sang outside. They believed the world was the same. Their lives undisturbed by the chaos. They went about their business, knowing that at the end of the day, they would return home, their flight unendangered. But so many lives had already crashed down.

Remy stood from his small bed. His bones cracked as he stretched and groaned. He looked out into the hallway. There was no sign of life. He glanced outside the window at the singing red birds and cursed at them. They had no fucking idea.

He opened a dresser drawer. Some underwear and socks. No undershirts. He glanced at the mound of dirty clothes near the closet. Would someone do his laundry? The service hadn't been running for a long time now. He might have to take a cab and go to a laundry mat. He cringed at that idea, but he needed clean underclothes. Otherwise, he would live in his robe. He didn't care. No one else did either.

Remy stood outside the bathroom and hoped it was clean. The other day, someone coated the toilet in brown, and it was left like that until the end of the night. Only because there were enough complaints from the few left living here, the toilet was cleaned, and the cleaning service came the next day to finish the job. The service only came two to three times a week now. He gingerly pushed the door open, hoping again not to see another horror show. Coast was clear, and he took a shower.

Remy returned to his room and made his bed. He kicked at the mound of dirty clothes and left the room. The television set was blaring from the community room. *It must be Jimmy*, he thought, and sure enough, Jimmy was parked in front of the television set in his wheelchair with that damn red hat on his head.

Jimmy leaned forward, gorging FOX News, and the aide behind him couldn't care less what was on the television set. He was too absorbed with Facebook or Twitter, or some other social media bullshit.

"Morning," Remy said.

"Remy." Jimmy didn't look at him. "He's gonna win. Just you watch. Four more years. Four more great years."

"If only I had some clean undershirts to wear. I'm running low on underwear too." Remy looked at the aide, who barely glanced at him. "I'm hungry," he said.

"Cafeteria's open." The aide turned in his seat, still focused on his cell phone.

Remy wanted to ask him if he even wanted to be here or if he was just here for a paycheck, but it wasn't even worth it. He missed the former staff. He missed Maria. She was one of the first to die, and that broke his heart.

Remy hated the walk to the cafeteria. He passed by so many empty rooms. After a while, they'd just stopped making the beds. Dirty clothes lay on the floor, some similar to his mound. They'd left Ben's chess set out on the table, stuck on its last move, and the radio in his room was still on. Remy couldn't walk in there, so the radio continued to play.

Near the cafeteria, Remy smelled something. Was there actually a cook instead of a delivered meal? He missed the cooked meals. When the virus hit, the kitchen staff left, and food was catered in. Not all of it was bad, but later, it got bad. He would run to the bathroom right after eating or later on in the day, and he would empty into the toilet. At least, during those times, the toilet had been decent, and he'd cleaned up after himself. He wasn't raised in a barn, but now, someone or someone's just didn't care.

"What's that smell?" He asked the lady standing behind the counter. She was always there except for Sundays and Mondays. She looked tired. Give it a little more time, and she would stop coming in all together. God only knows who would replace her. "It smells good."

"Chili." She turned, and the facemask caught her yawn. "Want some?"

"It depends. Where did it come from?"

"I made it," she replied.

"In that case, hell yeah." Remy picked up a plastic bowl and held it out to her. "What's the occasion?" He searched his memory for her name. She told him once or twice. He just couldn't remember anymore. "Sorry. Don't mean to be rude," he said.

"It was dead in here this morning." She looked shocked by her own comment. "I mean... It was very quiet this morning."

"Becky come out of her room?"

"No. She hasn't come out for a few days now."

"Anyone check on her?" The lady shook her head. "Can I have another bowl? I'll bring her some."

"Are you sure?"

What if Becky was dead? He handed the bowl to the lady. "I'm sure," he said, watching the chili fall into the bowl.

Going to Becky's room detoured him from his usual route. He was grateful for that. If he allowed himself to get depressed, he would never leave his room, and no one would check on him. They would leave him alone until they remembered he lived there, if they remembered.

"Becky?" Remy knocked on her door. "Becky, I have some food. Some napkins and plastic spoons. Becky?" He knocked again.

"Go away," she said from the other side of the door. Her voice was soaked in tears. "Just go away."

"Come on, Becky. You have to come out. You have to eat. At least use the bathroom."

"The bathroom is disgusting." She sounded closer to the door. "Just leave me alone. I don't want to catch the virus like the others did."

"I'm wearing a facemask." Actually, he had it shoved into his pocket. No one enforced it. No one cared. He put it on. "Come out and see. I'm wearing my facemask."

"You're not fooling anyone, Remy. Was Jimmy wearing his?"

He thought about it. "No," he said. "The staff was," or was he? "Come on, Becky. Come out."

"Go away."

"Fine. I'm leaving your food outside the door. I'm going to come back in a bit, and it better be gone."

"Or what?" She chuckled.

"Or I'm kicking your door down."

"You're an old man, Remy. You can't kick nothing."

"Oh, I will kick, and I will keep kicking. You hear me, Becky?"

"I hear you."

"Good, and it's chili. Homemade not delivery." He set the bowl by the door and placed the spoon on the napkin near it. He stepped away but stopped when he thought he heard the door open, and sure enough, Becky opened it just enough to pull the food inside. The door slammed shut. "I can't lose you too." Remy walked away.

There was a party going on outside, which gave Remy a chance to not think. He was tired of his thoughts, tired of the chaos. He sat in a chair by a window, and as he ate, he watched the party nearby. People were laughing and dancing. No one was wearing a mask. They hugged, held on to each other, and spun themselves around. It was like the virus never happened. How he wished that were true.

Watching them soon made him nauseous. He'd eaten most of his food, but he lost his appetite. They didn't get it, and most likely if they got sick, they would recover. Maybe he should let them in here, show them the many empty rooms, and see if reality hits. But they didn't give a shit, and he was so tired of people like them.

He headed towards the community room. Jimmy was still in front of the television set, watching FOX News. The aide was sleeping in his chair. There used to be a lot of aides. Now, they just had him, and he was fucking useless.

"Hey!" Remy said. The aide jolted in his seat, and Remy smiled. "Sleeping?"

"No." He rubbed his eyes. "Just dozing."

"Dozing? Well, while you doze, I'm going to take a walk outside."

"You can't go outside without supervision, and I'm watching Jimmy."

"Sure, you are. Have you checked on Becky?"

"Is she out of her room?"

"No." Remy leaned closer. "She hasn't come out for a while."

"I'm sure she's fine." The aide crossed his arms over his chest. "Anything else?"

"I need clean clothes," Remy said.

"Okay."

"So, when's the next laundry service?"

"I don't know. I'm sorry."

"Sure, you are." Remy stepped away. "I'm taking a walk."

"You can't go outside without supervision," the aide called after him.

"I won't leave the front yard." He thought he heard the aide say something else, but he didn't care. The man was pathetic, and it was disgusting that the facility only hired him. The administrator would not be back until Monday. She was useless too.

Remy opened the front door. He remembered the families that used to pour into the facility. Mothers, fathers, daughters, brothers, and the children. He'd hated their loud voices and laughter and screams. He would give anything to hear them again, but the families were gone. And they took who they could rescue away, and that wasn't too many. He had no one, but he would be damned if he let this virus win. Remy stepped outside.

One of the partygoer's cars was parked on the front lawn. They didn't care. They had to go to the party. They had to embrace living, the virus be damned. *Why not just drive into the fucking facility?* The car wasn't too far away from the building, but they must have known that nothing would be done about it.

Remy turned the other way. He didn't need to hear their music. He didn't need to see them dancing. He did not want to see them without facemasks. Remy made sure his facemask securely fit his face. He could not risk getting the virus, or it would kill him just like it did with the others.

Remy had hoped to see a regular neighborhood not just some stupid party next door. He wanted to see a mail truck, someone walk their dog, a bicyclist, jogger, something normal. Instead, he saw a black limousine parked in a nearby driveway, and a few cars parked in front of the house. A woman dressed in black stepped outside, holding one child by the hand. The other boy ran from her and looked at Remy. Both children were wearing black suits. Remy waved at the boy staring at him, and the boy flipped him the bird. Remy laughed. The kid had every right to be angry. The world was not fair.

The driver opened the door for the family. They got inside, and the limousine pulled out of the driveway. As it drove past him, one boy pressed his face against the window to look at him.

"Good luck, kid."

Remy walked back to the facility and looked at the building. What would he do if that place closed? Where would he go?

Out of the corner of his eye, he saw a woman walking along the street, pushing a cart full of plastic bottles. Her cane rested on a large black bag inside the cart. Pausing to catch her breath, she waved at him and smiled. No facemask, but it felt normal. He knew that it wasn't, and he waved back.

"The world's gone to hell. Four more years. Four more great years." He turned and spat on the sidewalk.

Remy entered the facility and closed the door behind him. The sound echoed down the hallway. If they didn't know he was gone, they knew he was back. Still, no one checked on him. He took off his facemask, shoved it into his pocket, and headed to his room. He'd seen enough for today.

A soft knock fell on his bedroom door. Remy opened it to see Becky standing on the other side. She was dressed, and her short, white hair was brushed back. She smiled and stepped into the room. He went to close the door but thought better of it.

"I don't want to be alone." She glanced at the mound of dirty clothes. "Mine is almost as bad as yours." She looked at him. "Is it okay if I stay in here for a while?"

He grinned and sat on his bed, and Becky sat next to him. "Are you okay?"

"No." Tears ran down her face, and Remy wrapped his arm around her.

"It's okay. It'll be okay."

"No, it won't," she whispered into his ear. "We're going to die."

He pulled her closer. "I'm not going anywhere, and neither are you. Do you hear me?"

Becky was quiet for a moment and then said, "I hear you, Remy."

He smiled and looked out the window. The red birds were back, singing that everything was okay, but everything was not okay. Things might not ever be okay, but if he had learned anything from all this, it was that he wouldn't give up.

"We don't give up," he said.

Becky squeezed his hand. "We don't give up," she repeated, wiping her tears away.

CAN HE FEEL OUR PAIN?

I did not want to go with my mother. I tried to get my brother to go with her, but he did not want to have anything to do with it. He stayed in his room instead, with the door closed and locked. My mother refused to go alone, so I finally agreed. And we rode the bus to the Port Authority.

It was cold outside, but we didn't catch another bus or a cab. We walked instead, barely saying a word to one another, and passed by boarded-up stores. Some had smashed windows. People sat in the streets looking lost. An argument raged from one of the open windows overhead, and something shattered. Was it glass, or another heart?

I stopped moving, but my mother walked on ahead of me. A long line stretched out before us. No one was following the social distancing rule. They didn't care. They all wanted to be here.

My mother fumbled in her pocketbook. I noticed some people watching her and moved closer. They probably didn't have tickets, and our tickets were expensive not only to get inside the Garden but to be on the lower level. My mother wanted to be as close as possible.

A staff person in a yellow shirt and black pants walked down the line, asking "Tickets?" and those with them took them out. The staff scanned the barcodes and escorted people to the front of the line.

My mother was led forward, but she stopped when she saw that I hadn't moved. She stepped back and grabbed me by the arm. "Come on," she hissed, and we moved to the front of the line. When we got inside, we joined another line.

Ten minutes later, I made it to the bathroom. My bladder was a knot, and my hands were ice cold. My hair was a mess. I stared at my reflection when I heard crying from the stall behind me. It was my mother, but it was also the woman in the stall next to her. Their sobs echoed throughout the bathroom. A moment later, they stepped out of the stall and looked at one another as if they were old friends.

My mother and I headed for our seats. The stage was dark. Two large screens hung on the sides and one above us for those stuck in the nosebleeds. No music. Just silence.

At seven p.m., a spotlight shined across the stage. A man dressed in black stepped out from the side. There was no podium for him or microphone in his hand. Instead, he had an ear set microphone.

The man surveyed the audience, his eyes settling on me. He watched me shift in my seat. Finally, he turned away and said, "Thank you for coming tonight, and thank you all outside for bracing the cold to be here with us now."

"Who is this guy?" I asked.

"Shush," my mother said.

"We all know why we are here." The man never gave his name. As if he read my mind, he said, "My name is not important. What is important is those we have all lost. They would be here today if he did not fail us."

His words brought about a lot of nods of heads, and one man sitting nearby cried, "He failed us!"

I jumped at the pain in his voice, which swept across the Garden. The two large screens and the one above us filled with images. Sick kids. People on ventilators. Black body bags. People crying at graves, and I flinched at one image of a young woman holding a rose over a tombstone. I felt him staring at me again.

The images disappeared, replaced with only one. It was the president with his smug expression and ridiculous hair. He did fail us.

"I want all of you to look at him." The man on the stage gestured to all the screens. "Focus on him."

I shifted in my seat again and glanced at my mother. The look in her eyes made my heart drop.

"Now, friends, those in here and those outside, close your eyes. Think of those that you lost. Remember them. Their face. Their touch. Their love. Let that fill you up."

The man sitting next to me trembled. The woman behind me sniffed. A sob escaped from my mother, and a tear ran down my face.

"Now, remember your loss. Being helpless. Watching them suffer. Having no choice but to lose them. Think of the empty chair in the kitchen. The space in your bed."

My hands curled into fists. My mother reached over and took my hand in hers.

"It makes you angry. Doesn't it?" The man asked.

"Yes," people whispered around me.

"I said. It makes you angry. Doesn't it?"

"Yes," the people said louder.

"Don't you want to rage? Scream? Scream so he can hear you?"

"Yes," everyone yelled including my mother, and my ears popped.

"Then close your eyes and focus on this man, our president, and feel. Feel everything. Your pain. Your loss. Now, send it to him. Focus and send it to him. Send all of it to him!" That last word boomed across the audience.

The man on the stage closed his eyes. My mother's eyes were shut. I was the only one looking at everyone and then at that image of him.

"This is ridiculous," I muttered. "Mom?"

My mother sat still with tears pouring down her face. She was still holding my hand, but she was somewhere else. She was thinking of him. They were all thinking of their lost loved ones. I could feel it. The hair stuck up on my arms and the back of my neck, and I couldn't pull myself free from my mother's hold.

My cell phone along with my mother's chimed. More rings and other notifications sounded off throughout the Garden.

I finally pulled my hand away from my mother and checked my phone.

My mother opened her eyes and checked her phone too. "Good," she said. "I hope he went to Hell."

MEETING WITH TOMORROW

I t was supposed to be an early spring. Seventy-degree weather all through March, but it was snowing. It was really snowing. The county roads were covered and slick, trees were falling down, and ice and slush was everywhere. The basement was freezing.

I set up the chairs, eight total. I turned the coffee machine on, and it bubbled, warming up, or at least trying to. I glanced at the clock on the wall. Would anyone show up?

Shortly after ten a.m., footsteps thundered down the steps and into the room. It was a few men, and they grabbed their chairs. A moment later, they jumped up and got a hot cup of coffee. I couldn't blame them. I was cold too, and a moment later, a middle-aged woman entered the room and sat on a corner seat.

"It's fucking cold down here," Jimmy said, and he zipped up his winter coat, shoving his hands into its pockets.

"When are the renovations upstairs going to be done?" Barnes asked.

"Soon," I said. "Maybe, by next month."

"Maybe, by then, they can pry our cold, dead bodies from the basement floor." Hall smiled as everyone else laughed. He looked over at the woman nearby, who was only wearing a hoodie and jeans. "Aren't you cold?"

"Cold?" Lesley asked. "What's that?" She pulled the hood over her head.

I thought we were ready to begin when small footsteps were heard going down the stairs. I turned in my seat to see a pair of white sneakers make their way toward us. It was an elderly lady that walked into the room.

"What?" She noted the look of surprise on everyone's faces. She shrugged and took a seat next to me. "Did you think that we were all dead?"

Jimmy turned and coughed.

Barnes opened his mouth to say something but then thought better of it.

"Would you like a cup of coffee?" Hall asked.

"Yes, please. Thank you." She watched Hall get her the coffee.

Lesley pulled at her hoodie. It was a bright red color. She quietly drank her coffee, glancing at the elderly lady every now and then.

"Thank you." The elderly lady took the coffee from Hall. "Amy. My name is Amy."

"Welcome, Amy." I clapped my hands together. The sound bounced off the walls.

"Was that really necessary?" Jimmy asked.

"Well, my hands are a bit warm now," I said. "Let's begin. We only have an hour. Who wants to go first?" I looked around at everyone, and my gaze fell on the empty chairs.

"Can you believe it's fucking snowing?" Jimmy rubbed his chin and then shoved his hands back into his coat. "No snow in February. March was like spring. Now, it's snowing. Nature is screwed up."

"It wasn't nature that made us sick." Barnes ran his fingers through his short hair and then reached into his overcoat, pulling out a pack of cigarettes. "You mind?" He asked me, and I shook my head. He put the cigarettes away.

"That was a year ago." Hall wiped some dirt off his black shoes. "Everything's still screwed up."

"Can you believe he was re-elected?"

"Lesley, no politics," I reminded her.

She finished her cup of coffee. "People just don't learn." She kicked at the cement floor underneath her.

"I finally moved out of my house," Jimmy said. "It took a long time. I never felt so much hostility in my neighborhood until the virus came."

"Did you say goodbye to your neighbors?" I asked.

"No. I left in the middle of the night with my family. House isn't sold yet, but we're not waiting. My neighbors want to try and raid it now? Go ahead. There's nothing left in there." Jimmy pulled his hands out of his coat pockets and crossed his arms over his chest.

"You shot one of your neighbors. Right?" Barnes asked.

"Yes, and I would do it again. Nobody asked them to break in and take my stuff."

"I saw a lot of gunshot wounds," Hall said. "When I wasn't treating victims of the virus, I was treating gunshot wounds and stabbings. We were so overwhelmed." A look of exhaustion crossed over his face but then disappeared a moment later.

"We were too." Barnes rubbed his hands together and then looked at the scars on them. "First, crime was down, and then it spiked. It was like purge night. Jails were becoming overcrowded. We had nowhere to put them." Barnes's hand fell over the pocket with the cigarettes.

"We had to let some of them go, and they did it all over again. They didn't care that they were killing people."

"I can't imagine being a doctor or cop during the virus," Lesley said. "But I remember the hospital when... When I lost my son." She focused on a thread sticking out of her jeans and pulled at it. "No one tried to save him. They just made him comfortable until he died. I couldn't let him go, so I followed them to the morgue. There were so many bodies." She ripped the thread out and dropped it to the floor. "So many black bags, and they were out in the hallway too. My son was going to be put into one of those ugly, black bags."

"You shouldn't have seen that." Hall placed a gentle hand on her leg, but Lesley turned away to wipe a tear aside.

"At the nursing home, we knew those black body bags very well. We knew that they were just waiting for us," Amy said. "Everyone died. Everyone except for me." She didn't look away when she said that. She looked at everyone in the room including me.

"Why didn't you die?"

"Jimmy!"

"What, Barnes? Someone had to ask."

"Why? So, you could put it on her tombstone?"

"Jesus, Hall. What kind of doctor are you?"

Amy's gaze sent a chill around the room, and it was still cold in here. "I watched my husband die. My sister." She looked down at her hands and played with a small diamond ring. "I lost all of my friends. The nursing home felt like a tomb, and I wanted to die." She gazed at all of us again, and I cringed in my seat. "I begged to die, but Death didn't take me."

"I wanted to die when I lost my son." Tears raced down Lesley's face, and Amy reached out and touched her hand. "I wasn't supposed to have children. That's what the doctors told me, but then I became pregnant. My son had asthma, and for ten years, he did not need an inhaler. Two years later, he got the virus. I never felt so helpless in my entire life. I can't go into his room. I just can't." She went to drink her coffee, but the cup was empty.

Hall took Lesley's cup from her shaking hands. "I saw a lot of people die. I wanted to save them. I tried to save them, but we ran out of supplies. But not the bags." He poured coffee into Lesley's cup and handed it back to her. He laid a hand on her shoulder and then returned to his seat. "He promised so many things but didn't deliver or delivered too late. I know no politics here, but I just want to say, he failed us. Mostly because he couldn't tell us the damn truth, answer a direct question. It really makes me angry." Hall's hands folded into fists.

"We're all angry," Barnes said. "I never felt so lost. I haven't been back to work since the quarantine. I don't have the heart for it anymore. Good people died, and the bad ones... Well, they seem to be everywhere. I don't want to save them."

"I'm lucky that my family and I are okay, but my children won't be the same ever again," Jimmy said. "One's just starting high school, and the other will graduate this year. And they won't look at the world the same way again. They don't trust those that are supposed to help us like the police and the doctors. No offense." He watched Barnes shrug and Hall sadly smile. "I don't know what kind of future is waiting for us, but it's broken. My children are broken, and I can't help them."

"Just love them." Again, everyone looked at Amy in surprise. "I don't believe love is the answer and can heal all, but we need it. We need to love, and we need to be there for whatever family is left. Otherwise, the virus won."

I glanced at the clock on the wall. Its hands were approaching the eleventh hour. "We're almost out of time," I said. "These meetings are good for us."

"These meetings are shit." Barnes aimed his empty cup at a wastebasket nearby and missed. "They don't solve anything."

"You could be like my family." Lesley looked at everyone. "They're lined up, waiting to see a therapist. They think I should see one too."

"Vultures," Amy mumbled.

"It's no surprise therapy suddenly became a booming business. All the damage. All the loss," Hall said. "We have to talk about it, or it will eat us up inside."

"I don't regret shooting my neighbor. He's lucky I didn't kill him," Jimmy said.

"I regret not quitting my job," Lesley said. "If I just stayed home, then maybe I wouldn't have gotten sick. Wouldn't have gotten my son sick."

"We don't know who brought the virus into the nursing home." Amy smoothed out her long, white skirt. "There was no way of not being exposed to that virus, and none of us were ready for it. But you would think that we should have been. Maybe he was the wrong man to run this country." She looked over at Hall. "But we're still here. All of us, despite the damage, despite the loss." She looked at the empty chairs, and her eyes teared up. "We're still here, and we have to find a way to live our lives, no matter how broken it is."

"I agree. Thank you, Amy. Same time next week?" I asked.

"Better not be in the basement again, or I'm not shaving my beard," Jimmy said as he stood up from his chair.

"Do you want to grab some lunch?" Lesley asked Amy.

"I would love to. Everyone seems to be giving me free meals just because I lived." She chuckled. "I do need a ride back to the nursing home afterwards."

"I'll take you." Lesley followed Amy up the stairs.

"Poker game tonight," Barnes asked Hall.

"I'm in." Jimmy walked with Barnes and Hall over to the stairs and playfully bumped into Barnes.

"Wise guy." Barnes pretended to hit him.

"Don't you have to ask your wife first?" Hall asked.

"Ha ha." Jimmy's laugh drifted down the stairs.

The basement quieted down. The cold chased away any lingering warmth. The chairs including the empty ones were returned to their spots. The coffee machine switched off along with the lights, and darkness moved back into the room.

But even in the darkness, Amy's words were still heard, "We're still here."

I WILL REMEMBER YOUR FACE

The children enjoyed the sunlight falling gently upon them. They laughed. They screamed. Their voices traveled rapidly, excited about a new day. Some kids chased each other, while others hung out on the horizontal ladder. Other kids kicked their legs out and swung high into the air. In a sandbox, a little girl made sandcastles, and a boy, maybe two years older than her, tore them down.

"Stop! Stop it!" Alex shielded what she could of what was left of her sandcastle. She failed. *Why was this boy being so mean to her?*

"Don't be such a baby." He pushed Alex aside and knocked over the rest of the sandcastle. "What are you? Five?"

"Nine. I'm nine. Aren't you a little big for the sandbox?"

"I'm eleven. Well, I will be eleven." He sat back and waited for her to build another one. "Three more years."

"Until what?" Alex scooped sand into a dome.

"Until I become just like them. Which one is your mother?"

"She's the one in the pink shirt."

The boy moved away from Alex, but only for a moment. He looked around. "There's two women wearing a pink shirt. What if the wrong one comes and takes you home? What if you don't realize it until it's too late?" He grinned at her.

"Jerk," but Alex stopped to look around. One woman was wearing a pink shirt, but it wasn't her mother. "I know my mother," and she resumed making her sandcastle.

"Are you sure?" He laughed.

Alex sniffed and wiped some tears away.

"Jesus. You are a baby."

"You're a jerk. Go play on the monkey bars."

"Don't be a racist."

"What? No. Can I just make my sandcastles? Is that okay?" She was almost done with it and moved closer to protect it.

"Go ahead." He leaned closer to her. "Finish the sandcastle."

"Forget it." Alex moved away.

"I promise I won't tear it down."

"I don't believe you. You're mean. Why are you picking on me?"

He was about to answer her when a commotion broke out behind them. He turned around, so did she. The adults were gathering around someone. Their facemask was green.

"Go," the adults screamed. "Take your virus and get out of here." Their voices demanded blood if she did not comply.

The woman in the green facemask stepped back. She snapped her fingers. Loudly. Twice. A boy jumped off the swings, hurried over to her, and took her by the hand. She glared at the adults. Only her eyes were visible. She stormed away, taking her son with her.

Alex sat back and finished her sandcastle. "She should not have been here if she was sick," she said.

"It's like Friday the 13th." The boy slammed his hand down on the sandcastle.

"Friday the 13th?" Some sand had gotten on her face, and she wiped it away.

"It's a horror movie. Well, horror series. Don't you watch horror?"

"Don't you watch the news? It's horrible."

"Anyway, Dad lets me watch horror movies, and we're living in the world of Jason Voorhees. Only it's not a hockey mask, and the mask changes color. You saw that woman. She was sick, and her mask was green." He stared down at the sand in front of him. "What are you waiting for? Build more."

"I'm done. I might go on the swings," but a girl grabbed the empty swing.

"You snooze, you lose." He laughed. "Anyway, speaking of my dad, I don't remember his face. What about you? Do you remember what your parents look like?"

"I'm not allowed to see their faces. One day, I'll have to wear a mask too."

"Until they find a cure."

Alex laughed.

"What's so funny about that?"

"They'll never find a cure." He punched her on the shoulder. "Ow! I'm telling."

"Baby."

"Jason!" He froze at his mother's voice. "I'm watching you."

"Your name's Jason?" Alex giggled.

"Shut up. Your name's Baby."

"Alex."

"I don't care. I don't play with babies."

"Well, you're playing with me, so let's build sandcastles. Jason."

He scowled at her. "I'm bored. Why do the adults bring us here? It's like punishment."

"Because it's the last freedom we have."

"You're such a nerd."

"I thought I was a baby."

"Whatever," Jason said.

Another commotion broke out nearby. He turned and bumped into her. She touched his hand, and they looked at one another. They glanced back at the figure with a dark purple mask, who was slumped over on a bench.

"Are they…"

"Yes," Jason said. "They're dead."

The adults panicked, running like a herd towards their children. The children were grabbed into their arms. Laughter turned into screams. Feet thundered across the dirt and grass. Voices pitched high, calling for children not found. Jason was ripped away. Alex was left alone in the sandbox.

Alex stood up and stared down at what remained of her sandcastle. She kicked it aside and looked at the figure on the bench wearing a pink shirt. She listened to the sirens in the distance.

Her father was already gone. They were coming, and they were going to take her away. She slowly walked over to the bench and touched the hand resting in her mother's lap.

She hesitated but then removed her mother's mask. She looked at her mother. "I will remember your face." She touched her mother's cheek and then sat on the bench, holding the mask and waited. "Will Jason remember mine?"

LIGHT DUTY

S unlight streamed into the office, falling across the computer screen. File cabinet drawers jutted open. Paperwork piled up. The keyboard flinched with the data entry. The nearby clock silently chewed the time away.

Heather paused in her typing. She looked at the stack of paperwork on her desk and sighed. Her eyes moved over to the clock, and she cursed at it. Then, she realized that she wasn't alone. A man in a nice suit sat in the corner, and he folded his hands in his lap.

"You don't have to be here." Heather placed a document in a folder and slid the folder into a file cabinet drawer. "I'm fine."

"I'm not so sure." He tried to meet her gaze, but she avoided his. "You don't have to be here."

Her coworker walked in and looked around the office. She glanced at the chair in the corner and then smiled at Heather, placing more documents on her desk. Her coworker left without saying a word.

"She thinks I'm talking to myself," Heather said. "One more week, and I'm done here." She stared at the stack of papers that was just placed next to her. "I'm ready to go back." Now, she met his gaze, and he smiled at her. But his smile was sad. "I'm good," she said.

"It was a bad day. It was a really bad day," he said.

"I know. I was there." She sat back in her chair, and it squeaked in response. She glanced at the door nearby. "One after another. They were all gone. You were the last one." She held his gaze. "Is that why you are here?"

"I want to make sure that you are okay."

"I'm okay." Heather placed another folder into a file cabinet drawer. "I just need to work." she said.

"If you say so." He smoothed out his gray tie and then folded his hands over his blue shirt.

"Your wife picked out a nice suit," she said.

"She always had good taste. You should talk to her."

"I have."

"No. The last time you spoke to my wife was at my funeral." He smiled at that.

She paused typing. "Why is that funny?"

"It just sounds so strange. My funeral. I never thought I would say such a thing, but here I am. With you."

"You could leave. You don't have to be here." She watched the door open, and another coworker peered in to look at her. "Hi. Can I help you with something?"

"No. Never mind." The coworker disappeared outside.

"They think I'm crazy. They hear me talking to myself. To you, but they don't know that you are here. Only I can see you." She opened her drawer and took out her pocketbook. Something rattled in her pocketbook, sounding like a bottle of pills, and she saw the look of alarm cross over his face. She placed a piece of gum into her mouth and put her pocketbook away. "It's just gum."

"Do you still have those pills?" He asked.

"No." She chewed on her gum. "It was a bad day. I wasn't thinking, and yes, I did something stupid. I took all those pills, and I shouldn't have done that. And if my brother hadn't found me..." She stopped chewing her gum. "I would be dead." She threw her gum into the garbage. "Now, I'm stuck in here, doing light duty."

"At least, you're not sitting next to me." He leaned closer to her. "You need to live your life, Heather. Be happy."

"I don't remember being happy. No one is happy especially not right now."

"Would you rather be dead?" He watched her flinch at his words. "The virus got me. It didn't get you."

"What do you want from me? Do you want me to give your wife a message for you? Tell your son something? He took losing you pretty hard."

"I said my good-byes, and I think they know that." He stood up from the chair and walked toward her. "I need to know that you are going to be okay."

Heather sighed and looked at him. "I can try." She smiled, and it wasn't a forced smile. "I want to do better, be better."

"That's all I ask," he said and started to fade away.

"Wait." She stood up from her chair. "Will I see you again?"

"I'll be close, and please, please do better, be better." He faded away.

"I will," she said. "I will." She returned to her desk and continued the data entry.

THE STRANGERS WE LET INTO OUR HEARTS

"All done here?"

"Just about." James smiled at the waitress and then turned toward the fireplace. He closed his eyes. The warmth from the fire felt good. "Guess I'll have that bill now." He looked at the waitress but didn't smile.

"I'll be right back." The blonde waitress stepped away.

James glanced outside at the darkness and shuddered. He looked around the restaurant and saw two men sit together at the end of the room. A family of six was near the fireplace. None of them were wearing facemasks. They all talked and laughed like this year was not a monstrosity. His eyes fell on the empty chair beside him.

"Here." The waitress returned, setting a slice of pumpkin pie down in front of him.

He tried to remember her name. She had said it when he was first seated at the table. *What was her name?* He looked at the slice of pumpkin pie. "What's this? I didn't order this."

"On the house."

He flinched at the look of compassion in her eyes. "Thank you, but I can't. I'm sorry."

"Don't you like pumpkin pie?"

"Yes, I love it, but…"

"It's missing something." She hurried to the kitchen and returned with a can of whip cream. She sprayed some on his pie. "Coffee?"

"Please. Thank you."

She disappeared back into the kitchen. He dove into the slice in front of him. It was thick, cold, but sweet, so very sweet. It was close to the one that his wife made. He almost had trouble swallowing the food down.

"You okay?" She looked concerned and placed the coffee next to the plate with the slice of pumpkin pie. "Something wrong with the pie?"

"No." He cleared his throat. "Thank you for your kindness." He tried to smile but couldn't. He stared into her eyes, looking for that compassion that was there a few moments ago. "Sit with me?"

"I don't know." She adjusted her black facemask. "We will be closing soon." The family of six gathered their things, said goodnight, and wished her happy holidays. "Oh, what the hell?" She sat in the empty chair, and he flinched. "Is this okay?"

"Yes. Fine. Thank you again for the pie." He finished his slice. *Stop thinking about your wife. She's not here anymore.* "Surprised you were open." He tried to steady his voice. "Thought I was going to be turned away when I got to your door, but the manager let me right in."

"He's a good guy," she said. "I'm Mary."

"James." He smiled, but his smile faded. "Some year. It kicked our ass pretty good." He could tell that she wasn't smiling anymore. Instead, a sadness filled her eyes. "Sorry."

"It's okay." She touched her facemask. "It's been some year, but it's almost over." Her eyes warmed up. "Your family in town?"

"No. My sons live a few hours away with their wives and my grand-children."

"Your wife?"

He dropped his fork into the plate. Its sound echoed throughout the restaurant.

"I'm sorry. It's none of my business."

"It's okay. She died," he said. "Last November."

"So, not from Covid?"

"Cancer. Last year was rough, and I didn't think it could get any worse. But it did." He felt her staring at him, waiting for him to continue. He looked at the fireplace but could no longer feel the warmth from the fire. "I can't see my family, even if I wanted to. Not until this damn thing is over with."

"I'm sorry." She reached for his hand but pulled back.

He forced a smile at her. "How about you, Mary? Got family here?"

"My daughter. She worked here earlier, so we were together."

"That's nice." He drank his coffee and then stared at what was left in the cup. "Cherish those moments." He looked at her. "If this year or last taught me anything, it's that time is valuable. We take it for granted." He watched the two men leave. "Some just don't get it until it's too late."

She heard the two men make a snide comment about the virus. "I'm done arguing with people. Let them do whatever they are going to do."

"I agree. Life's too short to fight. Anyway, how about that bill?"

"I'll get it." She moved away from the table but paused. "You're not alone. This is a good community, a good town, and there will be those to help you, if you need it."

"Like you?"

"Like me." She walked away and returned a moment later with the bill.

He examined the bill. "What's this? I wasn't charged for the pie or coffee."

"Both were on the house."

"No. No. I'll pay for them." He pulled out his wallet from his coat pocket.

"They're on the house," the manager said through his facemask. "Pay for the dinner. That's it."

He didn't see the manager exit the kitchen, but as fast as he was there, he was now gone.

"Thank you. Please, thank him," he said, staring at Mary. He put some cash on the table and made sure there was extra for Mary especially for her kindness toward him. "I hope it's not too cold out there. I have to walk home."

"Do you live far?" Mary asked. She didn't touch the money on the table.

"Maybe a mile or two. My wife... Well, she liked to drive everywhere. I really haven't driven since..." He nearly cried, and Mary placed a hand on his shoulder.

"I'll drive you." She picked up the bill and the cash from the table.

"No, that's too much. I'll walk." He moved away from the table and put on his coat.

"No," she said, surprising him with her firm voice. "I'll drive you. Just wait here." She disappeared into the back but returned with her coat and pocketbook. "Ready?" She asked.

"Yes and thank you again."

She laid her hand on his arm. "Happy Thanksgiving. Now, let's go." She moved towards the door but stopped.

"Something wrong?" He asked.

"What are you doing for breakfast?" She asked and watched him shrug. "Then, I'll pick you up at ten and we'll come back here for breakfast tomorrow. Sound good?"

Tears ran down his face. "Sounds good, and Happy Thanksgiving." He smiled, shaking his head.

"What?" She asked.

"I'm just a stranger," he said.

"And now, you're a friend."

James followed her toward the door but glanced back at the fireplace. *Let last year burn away. Let next year be better than today.*

The door closed behind them.

EVEN DARKNESS CANNOT SILENCE MIRACLES

The hallway was dark. The fluorescent lights flickered overhead. Shadows fell over the poster boards. The sound of whispering ventilators drifted down the hall with Donnette's sobs chasing after them.

She sat in a row of four chairs against the wall and hunched over in her seat. An N95 mask laid in the chair beside her. Her ears hurt from wearing the mask. Her hair was a mess. Tears fell on her shirt. She placed a hand over her chest as if to keep her heart from breaking inside.

"I'm sorry," she whispered. "I am so sorry."

She leaned back and rested her head against the wall. A sob lingered in her throat. She wiped her tears away, but more of them slipped down her cheek. The ventilators whispered down the hall.

"Hello."

She sat up in surprise and looked at the seat on her right. A little girl in a pretty green dress with her hair braided stared at her. She kicked out her legs, revealing white socks and black shoes. She smiled at Donnette.

"What? You're not supposed to be in here. Where's your mother?" The little girl pointed down the hall. "Your father?" She pointed in the same direction. "I'm sorry." The little girl's eyes teared up, mirroring Donnette's. "But there are no visitors allowed in here. If your parents ..." Donnette caught the sob in her throat.

"Why are you so sad?" The little girl asked, brushing her own tears away. She surprised Donnette with a bright smile, and her smile warmed Donette's heart. But Donnette shivered at the whisper of ventilators. "Why are you crying?"

"I'm sad." Donnette brushed a tear away.

"Why?"

"Because I can't save them." Maybe she shouldn't have said that. "I'm trying to save lives." *Fuck it.* "But I'm failing, and people are ..."

"Dying." The little girl turned in her seat and seemed to listen to the sound of the ventilators. "They're dying," she said and looked at Donnette.

"Yes. Dying. Why are you in the hospital?"

The little girl touched her hand. Her warm touch surprised Donnette, but she felt better and patted the little girl's hand.

"It's Christmas." The little girl smiled that bright smile again, but Donnette turned away.

"Is it? I barely noticed. Actually, I haven't noticed much lately." Donnette glanced down the hall.

"I have something for you." The little girl held a small black box with a red ribbon.

Donnette looked at her and then at the black box with a red ribbon. She shook her head, keeping her hands in her lap. "Where are your parents? Who brought you here? How did you get inside the hospital?"

The little girl looked down and pulled at the red ribbon, but she didn't undo the knot. "You're hurting my feelings," she said.

"I'm sorry." Donette reached over and touched the little girl's hand. "I like the ribbon," she said.

The little girl placed the black box with the red ribbon next to Donette's N95 mask. She looked at Donnette and smiled that bright smile again. "When you're ready, Donnette."

Donette looked down the other end of the hall. "I should find someone. Someone is probably looking for you. Wait. How do you know my name?" She turned back, but the seat next to her was empty. "Hello? Little girl?" She looked around the hallway, but she was alone. "Where did you go?"

She looked down at the black box with a red ribbon and slowly picked it up. The box was warm in her hands. She pulled at the ribbon. She didn't like that the box was black. Black usually meant death. She shuddered, remembering a poor soul, who was put into a black body bag earlier.

She removed the lid and lifted up a long silver chain. A large, silver heart hung from it. The heart had a good weight and shined brighter than the lights overhead. Something about it reminded her of her mother, and she didn't know why. But she put the necklace on, and it was like a warm embrace, a hug almost similar to her mother's. She hugged herself and cried, but not from despair.

"Thank you," she whispered. "Whoever you are. Thank you, and Merry Christmas."

ABOUT MELISSA R. MENDELSON

In high school, I lived in my notebooks. I needed to escape, run away from school, the world, and my family. I needed to live, but I couldn't. So, I needed to escape, but I didn't drown myself in my stories. I let go. I let my characters take me into their world, no matter how dark those worlds might be, and I followed each and every one of them until their stories end.

I have written so many, many short stories since high school, and I have met so many, many characters. Some of them are now lost to time. Others are floating around somewhere in the cyberspace, maybe still on Trigger Street, Hit Record, Gadfly Online, and other places, where they might still exist. A handful of them remain on paper ripped out of school notebooks and shoved into a dresser drawer because those are the stories that I want to tell one day. At least, I hope to in this world that is so uncertain and dangerous now.

2020 was uncertain and dangerous, and again, I needed to escape. But it wasn't just from the pandemic. I almost lost my left ovary that year, and the year prior, I had to decide to have a baby or never to have a baby. That choice was made in 2020, and I was not ready for the aftermath. But then Covid hit, and I was designated a front line worker by my job. And my father got really sick because someone failed to read his medical records and gave him the wrong medicine, which spiraled into a nightmarish situation that took up most of 2020 on top of everything else.

I needed to escape, and so many characters came to me, asking me to write their stories. Why should I write them? Who would want to hear them, but a lot of the characters were persistent. So, I let go. I let them take me into their lives, their worlds, and once again, I followed them until their stories end. And it is these stories that found home in the short story collection, Stories Written On Covid Walls.

The book trailer created by Space Dream Productions said it best, "Your story is not my story. My story is not your story. But these are our stories."